View from the top

I felt dizzy as I stared out across miles of green—the whole world rolled out to the horizon in one long green shag carpet. I towered over the other pyramids.

From up here, the steps looked even steeper. How would I get down? Clinging to the wall, I slipped into the little room built on top of the pyramid. Thick black soot darkened the walls and I crinkled my nose at the smell of the hot, dank air. I traced my name across the blackened walls, wondering if all this soot was left over from ancient prayers and offerings. I closed my eyes and whispered my own short prayer, "Please let eighth grade be different."

JUNGLE CROSSING

JUNGLE CROSSING

Sydney Salter

sandpiper

Houghton Mifflin Harcourt
Boston New York

www.hmhbooks.com

The text of this book is set in Bembo.

The Library of Congress has cataloged the hardcover edition as follows:
Salter, Sydney.
Jungle crossing/by Sydney Salter.
p.cm.
Summary: Thirteen-year-old Kat wants to be at "mini-camp" with classmates
rather than touring the jungles near Cancún, Mexico, on a family vacation, but
a story told by one of her Mayan guides helps her understand that by always
trying to please her friends, she is losing herself.

[1. Interpersonal relations—Fiction. 2. Self-confidence—Fiction. 3. Mayas—
Fiction. 4. Prejudices—Fiction. 5. Individuality—Fiction. 6. Vacations—Fiction.
7. Cancún (Mexico)—Fiction. 8. Mexico—Fiction.] I. Title.
PZ7.S15515Jun 2009
[Fic]—dc22
2009007974

ISBN: 978-0-15-206434-1 hardcover
ISBN: 978-0-547-55009-1 paperback

Manufactured in the United States of America
DOC 10 9 8 7 6 5 4 3 2 1
4500284959

TO MY PARENTS, DAVE AND RONDI,
who took me on my first Mayan adventure,

MY DAUGHTERS, EMMA AND SOPHIE,
who inspired me to write,

AND MY HUSBAND, MIKE,
who has supported me every step of the way.

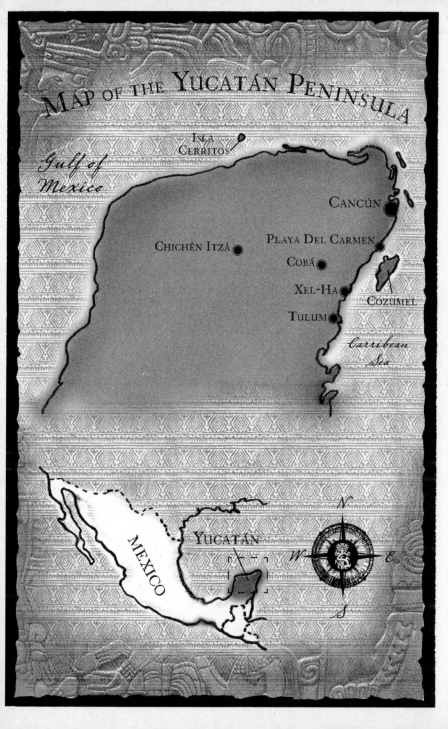

CHAPTER ONE

Hi! I miss you guys and we haven't even left yet.

Barb is already driving me nuts!

Remember to tell me everything that happens at mini-camp.

EVERYTHING!!!!

Love, Kat

P.S. Pickle wart.

. . .

I scanned the passengers for possible terrorists. Not the people with kids, or the blonde in the wedding veil, although it would make a great disguise. The guy in the seat across from us kept looking around the plane. Our eyes met. Wasn't he the guy they double-checked at security? I'd keep my eyes on him, just in case.

The flight attendant closed the door by turning a thin handle that looked like it could come flying open in midair, sucking us all out of the plane. I gripped my armrest as I imagined myself falling to the ground, whirling, whirling, splat. Thirteen years of life over. Just like that. My friends probably wouldn't even come to my funeral. They'd be too busy having a blast at Fiona's mini-camp, doing each other's nails, reading celebrity magazines, and talking about boys.

The engines made a loud grinding sound as the plane backed away from the gate. I looked out the window at the baggage carts racing across the tarmac, worried that my suitcase got left behind. Barb crossed her long, skinny legs and flipped through *Lost Treasures of the Maya*. The smell of her coconut sunscreen made me queasy. One little skin cancer warning from me, and she insists on wearing sunscreen on the plane. Maybe I shouldn't have shown her pictures from Dad's medical books. Nine is such an impressionable age.

"Do you think we'll find hidden jewels? I could become a famous explorer and travel all over the world and I'd be rich and on TV!" She sighed, looking down at a photograph of an elaborate jade necklace.

"Whatever." I closed my eyes. The cinnamon bun in my stomach churned as the plane approached the runway. Listening to the engines whir like a rickety old fan, I stared at the stain on the headrest in front of me. If Fiona were here, she'd say that the neon orange color on the headrests was oh-so '80s, in other words: old. Maybe technologically obsolete. The plane rolled onto the runway, vibrating like a wind-up toy as the engines sped up.

I held my breath and mentally said goodbye to Fiona and the rest of the gang, one by one. Then I added a special love thought to Zach B., even though he barely knows I'm alive.

"Why are you so sweaty?" Barb touched my forehead, then

brushed back her dark curly bangs and touched her own forehead. "I'm not hot." She fanned me with her book. "Mexico is going to be way hotter. Dad said."

"Just leave me alone." I breathed in for five seconds. Cinnamon-tasting acid burned the back of my throat. Pressure built painfully in my ears. I should've brought gum; I might end up with a raging ear infection.

"You're not scared, are you? I'm not. You weren't scared when we flew to Grandma's last time. Or the time we went to Disneyland either. Dad said airplanes are safer than cars. And—"

"I'm not afraid." I held my breath. I wasn't scared when I was her age either. But then I started junior high. Now I knew the truth: the world was a dangerous place, full of hurricanes, earthquakes, plane crashes, terrorist threats, bear attacks, contaminated food, bra sizes, mean PE teachers, cute boys who ignore you, and supposedly best friends who treat you like a tube of hairy lip-gloss.

The plane lifted into the air, making me feel woozy. I started breathing again, and I looked out the window as we climbed through the clouds, to make sure we didn't hit another plane: thirty-five percent of airline accidents happen during takeoff. The plane tilted. We're going down! I squeezed my eyes shut, but then the plane leveled. Guess we were just turning. I looked down through the clouds and watched as we passed over the soccer stadium. Wait! That house with the pool—were those small dots in the middle Fiona's Five? Had mini-camp started early? Oh. Wait. That was the rec center.

Barb shook my shoulder. "Are you still in a fight with Mom?"

I glanced at my parents a couple of rows back. Mom had gotten really mad at me last night after I'd presented her with my list of "34 Reasons Not to Go to Mexico" conveniently written in the travel journal she'd given me. She went on and on about all the sacrifices they were making for this trip, but they wanted to give us the opportunity to see a different culture, and we needed to spend time together as a family, and she and Dad needed to relax, and time is passing so quickly. Blah. Blah. Blah. She just proved my point by hitting upon reasons 3, 6, and 29 through 32 of why we *shouldn't* be taking this trip:

#3. You'll save a ton of money if I stay home

#6. I'm too old for family vacations (especially if it means missing mini-camp!)

#29. Barb will drive me crazy

#30. Mom will drive me crazy

#31. Dad will drive me crazy

#32. Why not make it a second honeymoon to improve your marriage? (And leave me out of it!)

When I showed her my list (and elaborated maybe a little too much on reason number 30), Mom ran into her bathroom and cried. So what? Missing Fiona's mini-camp was going to ruin eighth grade for me. But does Mom care? My head hurt when I thought about Fiona and everyone pigging out on pizza and root beer floats, swimming, watching tons of movies and staying up late, ranking all the guys in our class by looks, intelligence, and personality. And this year, Fiona's mom had hired some students from the beauty school to come over and do makeovers. And as much as my thirteen-year-old self needed to stop looking ten (boring straight blondish hair, barely visible bosom, four feet eleven and three-quarters), I wasn't just going to miss the makeover; I was going to miss all the little inside jokes that my friends would be talking about all year long. Like last year someone only had to say "pickle wart" and we'd all start cracking up. Inside joke.

But the biggest thing (and the thing that Mom totally didn't understand) was that Fiona invited only *five* friends to mini-camp. Being part of Fiona's Five meant instant popularity, always having someone on your side, never eating lunch alone, never hoping, hoping, hoping for IMs or phone calls. I'd be on the right side of all the gossip, invited to every sleepover, new movie, or shopping trip to the mall. But now she was thinking about inviting someone else!

On the phone last night Fiona had said, "Sorry, Kitty Kat, but you should totally skip your oh-so boring *family* vacation and come to *my* mini-camp. I totally have to invite five people, you know. Maybe Lexi . . ." I hadn't really listened to Fiona's list of replacements, because I was too busy picturing myself alone at my locker, alone in the lunchroom, alone at the school dance, alone on the weekend . . . Alone. Shut out. Reason number 33: eighth grade will be totally ruined.

As the plane reached cruising altitude, my stomach finally settled down, so I tore open my bag of M&M's and sorted them by color, eating all the yellow ones first, saving the green ones for last. Inside joke. Barb leaned over me, poking my leg with her sharp elbows, to look out at the clouds as the pilot announced a bit of turbulence.

"That cloud looks like a dragon," Barb said. "Oooh, and that one's a whale!"

Looked like big fluffy deathtraps to me. The plane bumped up and down. I tightened my seat belt until it hurt, wishing I had a shoulder belt too. I looked around to see if anyone else looked nervous. The guy sitting across from us bent down suspiciously to rifle through a grimy old backpack. He handed Barb a bag of Mini Oreos.

"You like?" he asked.

"Yes!" Barb ripped open the package.

Probably poisoned. I gave her a warning look and nudged her arm. You'd think she'd pick up on the whole taking candy, cookies, whatever, from a stranger thing. I flipped open my journal and added one more item to my list: "#35. Dangerous strangers."

"Oops. Sorry." Barb slapped her hand across her mouth. "Thank you for the cookies."

The man smiled and nodded as Barb bit into the probably poisoned Oreos.

Well, I tried.

• • •

Hi! We made it to Cancún! No plane crash this time. HA HA.
Wish you guys were here too.
Next year let's do mini-camp in Mexico.

Just kidding. HA HA.
Love, Kat
P.S. I have an idea—think of me at exactly
4 PM every day and I'll think of you too!

. . .

When I stepped off the plane in Cancún, the air was so hot and steamy that I almost couldn't breathe. Lush green jungle crowded the runway, adding an earthy smell to the lung-damaging jet fuel odors (I'd have to add that to my list). The sun beat down on us in a clear blue sky. All the blue and green looked kind of pretty, but I could practically feel the heat stroke coming on. Water. I needed bottled water. Regular Mexican water gives you dehydrating diarrhea.

While we waited in line, I pulled out my journal, nodding at reason number 24 (heat stroke), and adding new reasons. Number 36: lung-damaging jet fuel fumes; number 37: you can't drink the water.

Mom smiled, happy about me writing in my journal, until she saw the list. Her mouth crumpled into a frown, but then she cooed about the way Barb's damp hair curled up and charmingly framed her cherubic face. Mom actually used the word "cherubic." Good old reason number 30. Dad had a big smile on his face too—just one big cheesy family. We'd be the first ones targeted by bandits (number 8).

Barb grabbed Mom's hand and hopped up and down. "I'm so excited!"

My limp and stringy hair sagged in the humidity "oh-so

tragically," as Fiona would say. I grimaced at my reflection in the window; green vines grew out of my head, making me look like one of the creepy Mayan goddesses in Barb's book. I saw no sign of any white sand beaches or blue Caribbean Sea, only ratty vines and shrubs, like weeds on steroids.

People pushed against us as we got our luggage and waited in yet another line. Guys in white suits kept coming up and offering my parents "great deals" on resorts, as if we didn't already have a reservation. Bizarre! All the people breathing out germy breath, talking in loud foreign languages, and sweating stinky sweat added to the stifling heat. Barb stood in front of a big old-fashioned fan that sounded just like the plane's engines while customs agents searched through random suitcases. I did not want the whole world to look at my underwear. Or touch them. I'd have to do a wash right away. Fortunately, we made it through without being searched.

For some unknown reason, Dad was excited about the rental car, and he kept nudging Mom. It was kind of sweet to see them act excited instead of grumbling about work. Or about me. But still, they were getting on my nerves.

"A Grandpa Bug car!" Barb said. "It's so cute."

Mom started laughing. "Just like when we first got married."

"Yeah, real romantic," I said. "It looks a hundred years old. And I'm sure it doesn't have air bags." Frankly, I kind of expected something a littler nicer. What was the hotel going to look like? Their first crummy studio apartment in the worst part of town?

Barb and I climbed into the back seat while Dad crammed

our luggage into the tiny trunk. No seat belts. Dad's seat wobbled like a bobblehead as he sat down.

"Excuse me, but there are no seat belts in this vehicle." Ignored. "Mom? Dad? Did you hear me? Did you not listen when I told you about the number of auto accidents in Mexico? How am I supposed to survive if this tin can of a car doesn't even have seat belts?"

"Kat." Mom sighed. "Just relax."

"How can I relax if I'm about to die and never see my friends again?"

Mom sucked in a deep breath.

"We could play the silent game," Barb said.

"That's a great idea, sweetie." Mom leaned back and closed her eyes.

"We've got about a forty-minute drive to the hotel," Dad said. "Let's see if you can make it."

I took out my journal and added reason number 38: being asked to play ridiculous, childish games. Barb squeezed her lips shut and blinked at me rapidly; I wanted to smack her.

Mom leaned over and kissed Dad's cheek. "This is so romantic."

Barb clamped one hand over her mouth and motioned at Mom with the other. I turned my head and looked out the dirty window at the green rushing past. Where was the beach? We were driving into the middle of nowhere. A few crumbled buildings dotted the side of the road, but the rest was all poisonous, creature-filled jungle. I kind of wondered if we'd landed in the wrong city.

"Anyone hungry?" Dad asked.

"Yes," we all said.

I was starving: a bag of M&M's and three bags of airplane snack mix was all I'd eaten since breakfast. Dad pulled up to a shack on the side of the road. A woman and a little boy lounged in a hammock, laundry hung from a clothesline, and a sign painted in a first-grader's handwriting said GOOD EAT. And I thought Barb's lemonade stand had looked unsanitary! Were these people actually trying to make money? Selling food? Here? A big truck rumbled past, shaking the entire car with a whoosh of air.

"Dad, is this a restaurant?" Barb asked.

"It's fast food Mexican-style," Dad said.

Nothing looked fast about it, except the cars zipping past us, dangerously close.

"I don't know, honey." Mom frowned. "We can eat at the hotel right after checking in. Why don't we wait?"

"Nonsense. I want the authentic stuff," Dad said. "Paul and I always ate at these roadside stands. Great stuff. One time . . ."

I couldn't believe it. We're about to be crushed by a speeding semi, and here he goes again, rambling about his road trip through Mexico with his archaeologist friend, Paul. He acts like it happened last year or something—but it was, like, last *millennium.*

"Yeah, Dad. Um." I sucked in my breath as another truck flew past.

"One of the best tacos I ever ate was at a stand just like this—near Paul's dig site."

Mom shook her head and sighed.

The woman and boy swung in their hammock as if we weren't parked right there in front of them. Neither of them even looked at us. The clothes hanging on the line looked really old—like the kind of stuff we throw into the trash instead of giving to charity. A rickety-looking table held bowls of food, but where was the kitchen? I tried to peer into the dark door of the shack. Was that a real house? Or did they just work here? The taco carts at home looked so shiny and clean compared to this place—and I still wouldn't eat at them.

"I'm not touching any of it," I said. "If I survive the ride to the hotel, I don't want to die from some freaky food-borne illness."

"Let's just take a look," Dad said.

We all got out of the car. I figured I'd be safer standing away from the crazy drivers on the road. The woman swung her legs out of the hammock, looking tired and not all that excited about having a customer.

"Un taquito con frijoles," Dad said.

Flies buzzed all over the food. I could practically see the germs clustered on their twitchy little feet. With a crusty wooden spoon, the woman scraped the scummy layer off a bowl of black beans before dumping a glob onto a paper plate. She placed a handful of greasy rolled tortillas next to the beans and added a spoonful of thin red salsa. As Dad handed her a few bills of Mexican money, I crinkled my nose at the strange spicy meat smell. What was it made of? I glanced around for a menu, like a real restaurant—even a fast-food place—would have.

Nothing. I caught the thin boy watching me, and I turned away fast as a car full of normal-looking people drove past. In a normal-looking car. On their way to a real restaurant probably.

"*Gracias,*" Dad said, taking the plate from the woman. She nodded.

The food looked completely contaminated, but my stomach still rumbled as Dad dunked his *taquito* in salsa and gulped it in one bite. He held out his plate for me to try some. No way. I was waiting for normal food like I ate at home. Thousands of miles away.

"Mmm. Now, that is authentic," Dad said, crunching into another *taquito*. He ate three more.

CHAPTER TWO

Hi Guys! Mexico is so green and sunny.
Well, I'm off to the beach (with my sunscreen, of course).
Love, Kat
P.S. Remember to think of me at exactly 4 PM.
P.P.S. Remember to tell me EVERYTHING!

• • •

Rain. Big, fat drops of pouring rain. But that wasn't the worst of it. Dad was sick—nasty, disgusting sick. When he wasn't rushing to the bathroom, he lay there moaning. If only Mom had paid more attention to my list. Reason number 16: Montezuma's revenge.

I stretched across my bed, writing a postcard to Fiona. The picture of Playa del Carmen's white, white sand and blue, blue water looked nothing like the rainy gray day outside.

"What are you writing about?" Barb asked. "Dad barfing?"

"No, of course not." I lifted my pen and tapped my mouth. "I just don't want them to forget about me." Maybe they'd add one of my postcards to the mini-camp scrapbook. Fiona had kept a scrapbook of every mini-camp since the first one back in fourth grade. I hadn't been invited until last year, when Grace Williams went on vacation during mini-camp. She was shut out from the group all year, so she finally gave up and made new friends. But she wasn't popular anymore, not even close. I *had* to make sure Fiona remembered me!

Barb bounced onto the bed in her swimsuit. "Let's go swimming."

"It's raining," I said.

"So? You get wet when you swim."

Dad rushed into the bathroom again. Listening to that all day was going to make *me* sick.

"Okay." Risking a flash flood (number 20) was better than contracting Dad's disease. "We're going to the pool!" I yelled.

Mom poked her head through the door joining our rooms.

"You go and have fun," she said. "I'd better stay here with your dad."

I don't think she even knew it was raining.

That night, we walked through the fancy hotel garden—full of jungle plants, waterfalls, and squawking parrots—to eat dinner at the Mexican buffet place. Colorful red and green tablecloths and real flowers decorated all the little tables. Guys wearing crisp white uniforms rushed about picking up dirty dishes, bringing people clean plates, and sweeping crumbs off the shiny marble floor. A cute mariachi band walked around playing music, like at my favorite Mexican place back home. I headed right for the sizzling fajita bar—hot and, most important, fresh. But then I made a mini dish of nachos too. I loved having so many choices—and the dessert bar looked amazing. Three different kinds of chocolate cake! If only Dad had listened to us and waited to eat at the hotel, he could be enjoying all of this too.

Right after we sat down, Mom announced, "We've signed you up for a tour." She took a bite of enchilada (how did I miss those?). "Dad called Paul. He did his archaeological research in this area."

I dunked a tortilla chip into green salsa. "Like, duh. Dad can't stop talking about it." I've seen way too many photos of Dad's Big Adventure with Paul over the past couple of weeks—grinning from the tops of pyramids, digging into the dirt, hacking away at the jungle, drinking beer on the beach. "Preparation for *our* big adventure," Dad had called it. I was just traumatized by their shaggy and embarrassing facial hair.

Mom closed her eyes for a moment. "Anyway, Paul recommended the Ek Family Tours. It's an adventure tour for teens, but they also expose you to Mayan culture."

"Adventure? Wandering around the jungle, catching diseases . . . and Mayan culture? Would that include eating at disgusting roadside stands? No thanks. And who is this Ick family? I'm not doing anything with the 'Ick' family." I set my fajita back onto my plate. "I mean, do you even know who these people are? They could kidnap us and sell us into some kind of child slavery." Reason number 9. "I'm staying right here. At the resort. Where it's safe and clean." I watched one of the workers mop up spilled soda. "You can't make me go back out there. I'm sticking with the chlorinated pool and the free drinks."

"And ice cream," Barb added.

Mom rolled her eyes. "Paul stayed with the Eks while doing his doctoral research, and they've remained close. Paul told me the tours help the local people to preserve their heritage." Mom motioned to a waitress. "You'll get to see several Mayan ruins."

"Forget ice cream. We can find treasure!" Barb clapped her hands and began mumbling about gold and jewels and priceless statues while Mom ordered another margarita.

"Oh," Mom said. "I almost forgot the best part. Señor Ek invited you to his granddaughter's birthday party—apparently it's quite a big deal."

"Apparently the girl doesn't have any real friends." I scoffed. What kind of loser invites strangers to her birthday party? Who would I invite to *my* next party if I was kicked out of Fiona's Five? "Mom, this whole thing sounds disastrous." I didn't want any part of this deal. We'd end up like those stupid tourists they're always showing on cable news—held for ransom, or worse! I had to get us out of this; Mom had obviously lost it.

"Wait, Mom. You said a teen tour. Hello? Barb isn't a teenager."

Barb smirked at me. "So? You've only been a teenager for three days."

"Four. Today's almost over." I turned thirteen the week after school got out (and had a slumber party that even Fiona called "oh-so funtastic").

"Girls," Mom warned. "Señor Ek personally made an exception for Barb, since Paul is almost like family to him—and us. I trust Paul completely."

"Yippee," Barb said.

"Great. I'll be the only one with a dorky kid tagging along. But maybe they'll kidnap her instead of me."

Barb's eyes welled up with tears, and Mom shot me a sharp look.

"I hope your dad will feel better in a couple of days," Mom said. "Then we can go sightseeing as a family."

"Maybe we should go home." I could get there just in time for mini-camp. I smiled. Maybe I could avoid Grace Williams's fate after all.

"We're not going home," Mom said. "Dad will recover, and everything will be back on schedule."

"You could just send me home," I said, ignoring Mom's sad eyes.

• • •

PLAYA DEL CARMEN, HOTEL MAYA

Hi! I'm going on this special teen tour. Sounds pretty cool.

Nice to ditch the parentals and meet some cute guys.

·17·

How did you guys rate Zach B.? Did the french fry incident lower his score?
Love, Kat
P.S. 4 PM
P.P.S. Remember EVERYTHING!!!

. . .

The next morning, we waited with some other people in the airy hotel lobby for the "Ick" Family Tour. We heard the bus rattling around the circular driveway before we saw it. It was an old school bus painted with huge murals of parrots, Mayan ruins, warriors with feather headdresses, and a big jaguar on the front. The door opened and a twentysomething guy with long black hair and dark skin jumped out. He looked kind of like the suave assassin in that Spanish movie Mrs. Ruiz showed us the last week of school. Hair: 8.5. Face: 8.7. Smile: 9. Possibility of being dangerous kidnapping stranger: 9.9. Remember it's the cute ones that really fool you. He read names off a list.

"Katherine and Barbara Crosby?" he said with a thick accent. "Señor Paul's *amigas*." Charming accent: 8. "Welcome, welcome, *bienvenidas*!"

"Thanks, I guess," I said. The guy was a little *too* enthusiastic.

"I saved a seat up front for you." He swung his hair over his shoulder. Okay, maybe his shiny black hair was a 10, but he still looked kind of dangerous.

"Oh, goodie!" Barb said.

A thousand butterflies fluttered in my stomach as I climbed

aboard this strange bus with a possible criminal. We should just fly home. I could go to mini-camp, and Dad could recover in the safety of his own home. After everyone got on the bus, I looked behind me. Three girls about my age sat on separate seats—one had long blond hair with electric blue highlights. Behind me, a boy who looked a grade or two ahead of me sat with his younger brother, who was hunched over a video game. A pair of pale blond girls sat together near the front.

In the last seat sat a true Bronze Sun Goddess. She had a dark tan, and her hair was done in gobs of tiny braids with silver beads on the ends. They brushed against her bare shoulders when she moved her head. Sure, she looked good now, but in twenty years she'd be covered with skin cancer lesions and wrinkles. Right? Two guys sat backwards in the seat in front of the Sun Goddess—speaking French. Even from behind I could tell the guys were perfect 10s. In looks anyway.

The bus started with a bang and chugged out of the driveway. Of course there weren't any seat belts.

"Okay, everyone," the tour guide said. "*Buenos días. Me llamo Alfredo.* We going to have real good time today. Today we kayak in beautiful Caribbean and snorkel. See many fish."

Yeah, but how many sharks, jellyfish, and barracuda? I thought of all the dangerous creatures on my list. Swimming with all the germs in the hotel pool was bad enough, but at least they didn't have big teeth or deadly stingers.

A couple of the girls in the back started giggling and imitating Alfredo's accent.

"Let's go. *¡Vámonos!*" Alfredo said.

The bus wound through the streets of Playa del Carmen,

hitting pothole after pothole. I saw some cool-looking souvenir shops, and tourists wearing hideous floral shirts, and even though some of the old brick buildings might be fun to sketch, everything looked like it could use a good coat of paint. As the driveways to the resorts disappeared, all we saw was jungle, with an occasional dirt path leading off into who knows where. I rested my head against the window, watching the road ahead of us. Nothing but gray pavement winding through a tunnel of green, except for a kid standing alone on the side of the road. Not a taco stand in sight. What could someone be doing in the middle of nowhere?

As we approached, the bus slowed. Great, Alfredo's thinking about picking up a hitchhiker! Doesn't he know it could be a trick? Bandits could be hiding in the bushes, waiting to attack. I sat up, peering through the dusty bus windshield, looking for movement in the jungle. The bus actually swerved to the side, pulling up next to the kid/hitchhiker/possible bandit. The door swung open, and the kid—who seemed about my age, but was really short, like me—climbed aboard, frowning and looking kind of scary. I attempted to imitate Fiona's don't-mess-with-me glare, like I did while walking past suspicious guys on the plane. I kept my eyes on his hands until he caught me looking and sneered at me. And then I glanced away, cheeks burning. It only got worse when Alfredo announced, "My cousin Nando, everybody." Alfredo clapped his hand on Nando's shoulder. "Give a big *bienvenido!*"

Mangled Spanish greetings echoed throughout the bus.

Nando scowled and avoided Alfredo's eyes as he slumped

into the seat across from Barb and me. This guy was Alfredo's cousin? Pretending to fix my hair, I snuck a glance. No way. His body was only a 3. Plus, he had an angry look on his face, like one of those carvings in Barb's *Lost Treasures of the Maya* book. Personality: 0.2. Points just for breathing. Inside joke. Alfredo said something to him in Spanish, except it didn't sound like anything Mrs. Ruiz had taught us in fifth period. And I'd gotten an A in the class. I listened hard for familiar words. Nothing. Were they talking in some code? Were we really about to be kidnapped? Nando looked out the window while Alfredo eased the bus back onto the road.

Barb leaned over to me. "Do you think he's a real Mayan?"

"Why would I care?" I could hear the girls behind me talking and getting to know one another. I wished I'd had the guts to sit with them, but that girl with the blue hair looked "oh-so fashion daring," as Fiona would say, and the others were probably in high school. Still . . . Nando kept looking at me, making me nervous.

"Let's go sit back there," I said.

"No, we have to sit here. Alfredo said."

I shoved Barb. "Well, I'm old enough not to have to sit by the teacher, like some total freak. I'm moving."

Just then Alfredo called over his shoulder, "So you know Señor Paul?" I watched him flash a bright smile in the wide rearview mirror, but I still didn't trust him, not one little bit.

Barb leaned forward in her seat and launched into a fifteen-minute explanation about the books Paul gave her about Mexico, about how his family always comes to our house for

Thanksgiving and then for Fourth of July, and he has a girl about her age, but she doesn't even like treasure hunting. Blah. Blah. Blah. Alfredo talked about how Paul always visited *his* house after the New Year, and how his little sister loved to explore old ruins and wanted to be an archaeologist someday.

"Me too!" Barb practically shouted.

I considered jumping over the back of my seat, but the bus bounced so much that I'd end up falling into the aisle and looking like roadkill.

"Why do you keep looking at me?" Nando asked.

"I'm not." I scrunched low in my seat, pulling my knees to my chest, hoping that Nando with his combined score of 3.2 wouldn't try to talk to me again. I was *so* not trying to look at him, but I couldn't look out the window the *entire* time. A few minutes later I risked glancing to the back of the bus and noticed that three of the girls had scrunched together. I could hear them talking in fake Spanish accents and bursting into giggles. It reminded me of the time Fiona's Five went to the mall and we spoke in English accents all afternoon. To the loo! Inside joke. If I concentrated really hard, maybe I could transport myself back home, where mini-camp was barely starting. Fiona's mom had probably bought Krispy Kreme doughnuts.

The bus clunked along a sandy road to an empty beach where palm trees grew at angles out of the sand and hammocks swung between them in the breeze. Barb's coconut sunscreen smelled good here.

"Okay, everyone," Alfredo said. "First relax, then kayak, then lunch. Okay?"

As we got off the bus, the other girls ignored me. Next to tall-for-her-age Barb, I'm sure I looked like another fourth-grader. I don't know why Mom won't take me to get tested for hormone deficiency or delayed puberty. I'm like the only one without breasts—here, at home, everywhere. Maybe being devoured by a shark (reason number 18) would be better than returning home a total loser. I scanned the horizon for fins and saw Barb splashing in the water with the blue-haired girl. I should have warned her about jellyfish.

Two of the girls stood next to each other making little motions with their hands.

"Jessie! You cheer?" the taller one asked.

"Yeah. I'm missing a ton of practice this week," Jessie said.

"Me too."

"We could totally practice together, C.C." Jessie made a big C motion with her arms, then switched to the other side. "C, C," she said.

"You're so funny." C.C. giggled.

Okay. Whatever.

The Bronze Sun Goddess shared a hammock with the two guys. She looked like she was my age, but just barely, and she *could* be a swimsuit model. The guys both had the right amount of muscles when they took off their shirts. The quiet girls walked along the beach picking up shells, and the two brothers threw pebbles into the water close to Barb and the blue-haired girl.

I closed my eyes and breathed in the smell of the warm salt air and listened to the waves roll onto the beach. Despite reasons number 1, 9, 18 through 21, 23, and 28, this really looked like a postcard of paradise.

Too soon, Alfredo gathered us together on the beach. "Okay," he said. "Who does sea kayak before?"

The brothers raised their hands.

"Try speaking a little English, why don't you," the blue-blonde said in a low voice, and the cheerleaders giggled.

Nando squeezed his eyes shut for a moment and muttered something.

Alfredo showed us how to paddle and pointed to a small red buoy out in the sea that marked the coral reef. While the guides dragged long, flat plastic sea kayaks onto the sand, we picked out snorkeling equipment. I stared into the water-filled barrels, the perfect breeding ground for thousands of germs. Everyone else grabbed a mask and snorkel and headed over to the kayaks as I peered at a chunk of something floating in the water— probably a huge germ colony complete with condos and multiplexes. The water even smelled bad. Not cleaning-solution bad, but horrible-vomiting-disease-like-Dad-had bad. I looked over at everyone climbing into the kayaks. Most of them held two people, but a few were singles. Nando shook his head at me, walked over, plucked a snorkel and mask out of the water, and handed it to me. The rubber felt slimy with bacteria.

"You ride with me." Alfredo motioned to Barb. "See the most fish."

Barb hopped up and down in her flippers like a little frog. "I'm so excited!"

Lucky I didn't have to ride with him! His accent did make

him sound kind of dumb, but then again, with the hair and the smile, he was still at least an 8.5. The Sun Goddess and the Hunky Blond paddled off in a double kayak. I stood by a bright yellow one, struggling to slip the flippers onto my feet. The blue-blonde glanced around. I smiled at her, kind of like an invitation to join me, but she ignored me and climbed into the last double kayak, waiting for the other perfect 10.

"Everybody in," Alfredo said. "Let's go."

Alfredo swiftly turned his kayak and headed toward the buoy. As I sat down in my single kayak, the seat burned the backs of my legs and I could practically feel the skin cancer growing on my shoulders. I shoved off with the paddle, but the kayak stuck on the sand. As I climbed back out, my flipper got tangled in the paddle's safety rope, so I hopped on one foot, trying to get free as my kayak slipped into the water—with my leg in it. The blue-blonde laughed and pointed, so of course everyone had to turn and look. And that's when I fell. Face-down, gagging on salt water, possibly drowning, with my foot hanging in the boat and my butt flying in the air. What an embarrassing way to die.

CHAPTER THREE

I lifted my head out of the water right as a small wave hit me. I choked and coughed as the salt water burned my throat. Nando paddled back and helped me into the boat—actually touching my arm.

"You use fins for snorkeling, not paddling," he said, not in a nice tour guide way.

I grabbed the paddle from his hand. "I know that."

He raised one eyebrow as if he wasn't quite sure. "*¿Estás lista?* That means are you ready?"

"I know that too," I mumbled.

Nando shook his head as I shoved my paddle against the sand as hard as I could. But the kayak wouldn't budge. So he reached over and pushed me hard with his hand. As soon as I'd drifted a bit from the shore, I dipped my paddle into the water. My arms burned as I paddled as fast as I could, but my kayak kept turning in the wrong direction. I almost did a 360.

Nando laughed at me. And then he shouted directions in Spanish, but we didn't learn those words in Mrs. Ruiz's class. Tears pricked my eyes, which already stung with salt water. *Why am I doing this?* I wondered. Everyone else was out at the buoy, jumping into the water and snorkeling by the time I'd even started paddling. I didn't even want to swim around all those sharks and who knows what else. Tears welled in my eyes. I just wanted to be reading magazines and thinking about Zach B. At Fiona's house! I thought about how Fiona had spread rumors about Grace Williams's crush on Quinn Courtland—just because she'd missed mini-camp. She wouldn't do that to me, would she? I slapped my paddle back into the water.

"You have to paddle on both sides." Nando floated back to me. "Right. Now left. Now strong on right."

"I know." I felt like a complete idiot.

"Doesn't look like it."

"I mean I know that *now*." I paddled twice on my right side—just so he couldn't see my face, hot and itchy as if sunburned—and bumped into Nando's kayak.

"Whoa!" Nando nudged my kayak away with his paddle. "You paddle on one side, then the other side. Left. Right." He talked really slow, as if English were *my* second language!

"I think I've got it now," I said as we got closer to the buoy.

Nando shrugged and totally showed off by zipping ahead, tying up his kayak, and diving into the water—all before I reached the buoy.

After I finally tied my kayak to the others, I just sat there with the sun beating down on my shoulders and my already-hot-from-embarrassment face. My head kind of ached. Isn't that the first sign of heat stroke? Reason number 24. I watched the others bob around in the open ocean in groups of two or three, their snorkels sticking up in the air, reminding me way too much of sharks. The water seemed kind of choppy. One of the girls kept lifting her head out of the water to cough. I didn't want to choke on seawater again. My throat still kind of hurt from falling in before. But then the blue-blonde pointed me out to Barb.

"Jump in! It's amazing!" Barb called. "So many cute little fishies!"

I took a deep breath. I couldn't be the *only* one who didn't snorkel. Even old ladies go snorkeling. I'd bragged to Fiona about snorkeling. I had to do it.

I set the snorkel down by my feet; no way was I sticking that thing in my mouth.

And I jumped in.

The water felt nice and cool, but my mask was all foggy from hanging around my sweaty neck, so I could barely see anything. Plus, I had to keep popping my head out of the water to take a breath. Yikes! What just brushed my legs? I rinsed off my goggles, put them back on my face, and swam around near the kayaks. Dead coral lay scattered on the bottom like bones, kind of creeping me out and reminding me way too much of my social life. I swam toward a purple fan coral and watched a school of black angelfish float past, wondering if fish had social status. Like was the last fish in the group the loser fish? I spotted a huge coral that looked like a giant brain. If I *had* a brain, I'd be back on the beach, in the shade. A toothy-looking eel slipped into a rocky hole beneath me, so I quickly swam back to the surface. Near miss. Barb motioned to me about a school of blue and yellow fish, but I ignored her.

Alfredo shouted, "Back to the beach, everyone."

Finally!

Almost everyone was swimming near the kayaks, and the two brothers had started to paddle back. Alfredo boosted Barb up before lifting his lean, muscular body into the boat and heading to shore. I swam to my kayak, took off my mask and fins, set them on the seat, and reached over and pulled the paddle rope. *Smack.* The kayak flipped. My snorkel and fins drifted down to the bottom, right near the eel rock. Nando stared at me.

"I'd get them, but there's a big—"

Nando huffed, *"Turistas,"* flung his wet hair back from his face, and dove down to the bottom, flipping my kayak back over on his way up. He tossed my mask onto the seat, then swam to his kayak. I struggled to pull myself up. Nando just watched! After about eight tries I scrambled into the kayak, scraping my knee. Great. Blood attracts sharks. Balancing myself carefully to avoid falling back into the water as bloody shark bait, I started to paddle to shore, left then right, and bumped into the Sun Goddess.

"Watch out, *chérie,*" she said in her fantastic French accent.

"Sorry."

"No problem," she said.

But the Hunky Blond looked at me like I was a big fat zero in looks, intelligence, and personality. I paddled so hard my arms felt as if they would break like that dead coral, and I still got there last. Everyone huddled in a little thatched hut eating fruit.

"Kat, the pineapple is so yummy," Barb said.

"Yeah, but is it washed?" I thought of Dad vomiting every five minutes.

Barb shrugged, then went on a ten-minute undersea travel-ogue. "Did you see the skinny fish? The black ones? The yellow ones with white?"

No. No. And no.

"Oh, oh." Barb waved a piece of fruit at me. "Alfredo told me all about his cousin's birthday party. It's going to be amazing."

"I truly doubt it."

We spent the rest of the afternoon lying on the beach or pairing up in the hammocks. I swung in a hammock by myself, not saying anything, like a big old nobody. I'll be a nobody back home too—on the outside of every inside joke. I pictured Fiona's Five sipping sodas by her pool, probably talking about me behind my back, rating my body parts the way they rated Grace Williams's wardrobe last summer. Lunch-box shirt. Inside joke.

Everyone else chatted away. The Sun Goddess—Monique—was from Paris. The Hunky Blond Dante, lived in Belgium. Luc, the other Sun Goddess admirer, was from Germany. The brothers Josh and Max came from New Jersey.

The blue-blonde who laughed at me but thought Barb was the cutest thing ever, lived in New York City. Her name was Talia, and she went on and on about how the clubbing in New York was far superior to Cancún and Playa. Yeah, right. How old was she, fourteen?

The cheerleaders flipped all over the sand showing each

other their moves, while the others talked about music. Talia claimed to have seen almost every concert in existence.

At mini-camp they'd be lying out by Fiona's pool, rating guys. Luc and Dante would score perfect 10s. Nando would get a big fat 0 for personality because he'd sat in his stupid kayak and watched me suffer. My dad was even paying him! I reached into my backpack and pulled out my journal and added two new reasons. Number 39: scary eels. Number 40: mean tour guides. Talia watched me, so I quickly flipped away from my list and sketched a few palm trees.

"I like to draw sometimes," she said. "You know really the only way to learn to draw is to study the masters. Like in New York they have all these amazing museums—filled with all the most famous paintings in the world—like you wouldn't even believe it. The only place to live if you want to be a really famous artist is New York City. Like I'd totally take a drawing class, except I'm so busy and—"

I stopped listening and worked on getting the shadows right in my sketch.

When we finally got on the bus again, everyone sat near the back, talking about movies and comparing American and European TV shows. Once again, Talia, flipping her blue-blond hair around, was the expert. I thought about sitting back there, but . . . *Bock! Bock! Bock!* I chickened out and sat with Barb, right behind Nando. Alfredo tuned the bus radio to some funky Mexican music and bobbed his head to the beat. Dancing: 3.5. He and Nando shouted to each other in their bad Spanish.

"Do you think there's treasure buried in those trees?" Barb

pressed her face against the window. "I'm going to ask him."
She nodded to Nando.

"No, don't." I put my hand on her outstretched arm. "You'll
just make him mad."

"But I want to say something Spanish—like I can say please.
I mean *por favor.*"

I leaned toward Barb. "His Spanish isn't all that great. I'm
pretty sure Mrs. Ruiz would flunk him. His English is okay,
but still, don't bug him."

Nando whipped his head around. "I wasn't speaking Spanish. I was speaking Maya. And my English is good. *Mi profesor,*
my teacher—"

"I know what that means."

Nando shrugged. "*Mi profesor* gave me high marks. I'm not
a dumb Mexican, like you American *turistas* think. I speak three
languages. How many do you speak?"

"I didn't think you were dumb." I felt my face flush as I
lied. "But you are a Mexican because you live in Mexico."

"I am Mayan, son of kings."

"Well, then I'm a daughter of European warriors, or something." I could never get a straight answer from Mom or Dad
about my ancestors. Half seemed to be English; some came from
Scotland, I think. Or Norway or somewhere cold like that.

"Did the kings have treasure?" Barb asked. "Is there still
treasure out in the jungle?"

"Why?" Nando narrowed his eyes. "You want to rob our
temples so you can put our culture in a museum far away?"

Barb's eyes filled with tears. "I just want to be a famous explorer like my dad's friend Paul."

"Don't let him bother you." I put my arm around Barb and gave Nando a piercing look. "He's just making that stuff up. He has no idea about his ancestors. Plus the Spanish conquered all the Mayans and Aztecs a million years ago." I shot Nando another look. "I learned about that in fourth grade." I patted Barb's shoulder. "You'll learn all about it next year."

The girls in the back started singing pop songs, reminding me about the time Fiona sang on the escalator at the mall so we'd all chip in and buy her a pair of earrings. Why hadn't I just sucked up my fear and sat with them? I could've told them about how the security guard told Fiona to "settle down or suffer the consequences," so she made us buy her two pairs of earrings.

"Your American teachers don't know anything." Nando glared at me. "You think just because the Maya stopped making big buildings, they're all gone."

"Is the treasure all gone?" Barb asked with a bit of a sniffle.

"There are many treasures left to discover," Nando said. "Archaeologists like Señor Paul find new ones every day."

Barb lifted her chin and looked straight at Nando. "Are you mad at Paul?"

"No. He's okay. But I still think my people's treasure should stay right here in Mexico. It belongs to us."

"I promise to give you all the treasure I find," Barb said. "And I'll tell Paul, I mean Señor Paul, to do the same thing."

Nando fought a smile.

"Whatever," I muttered. Little suck-up. I looked out the window at the tangled jungle of low trees, wondering if that pile of rocks we'd passed had once been a temple or something.

Barb glanced out the window. "How do you know where to look? Is there treasure right there?" She pointed.

"No. They're building another stupid hotel." Nando rolled his eyes. "We know about our treasures from old stories, ruins, and—"

Barb leaned forward. "Do you know any stories?"

"I'm not going to waste my stories on American *turistas*."

"Please? I mean *por favor*. I promise not to tell anyone," Barb said in a low voice. "Promise." She pretended to lock her lips with a key. Should I remind her about the time she told Fiona that I didn't really need a bra?

"Yeah, you're real good at keeping secrets," I said.

"Kat has to promise too, right?" Barb scrunched her nose at me.

"Don't worry. I'm not even listening." I leaned back and closed my eyes. If only I'd ignored reason number 8 (bandits) and brought my iPod anyway.

"Sometimes I make up stories—like the ones *mi bisabuela*—"

"Great-grandmother," I interpreted.

Nando shot me a look. "Like I said before being interrupted, I make up stories like *mi bisabuela* used to tell. Except I add more adventure."

"Oh, that's my favorite kind!" Barb jumped up and sat in Nando's seat. "Tell me!" she said about a hundred times. He fell for her cutesy routine—just like Dad always does.

Nando began, "Long after the gods created the Mayan people out of maize, that means corn—" He shook his head at me.

"Duh," I said under my breath.

"Yet long before the Spaniards came to destroy their kingdoms . . ." Nando continued.

"Wait," Barb said. "Why are the Mayan people made of corn?"

Nando sighed. "Are you going to interrupt with questions the whole time?"

"Just this one. Promise." Barb closed her lips tight.

"The gods wanted to create creatures who would worship them. First they made the animals, but they couldn't talk. Then the gods created people out of mud, but when it rained, they fell apart. Then the gods created people out of wood, but they had no feelings, so the gods washed them away in a big flood. Finally, the gods created people out of corn, and they turned out just right." He turned around to look at me again, but I whipped my head back to see why everyone was laughing. Monique crossed her arms across her chest because her boobs had been bouncing all over the place. At least I didn't have to worry about that, but my stomach felt like it was jiggling its way up to my lungs, causing some sort of irreparable damage.

"Corn is my favorite vegetable," Barb said. "Now the story. *Por favor.*"

"Many hundreds of years ago, during a booming thunderstorm, a baby was born to a wealthy elite family in Cobá. The priests named the baby Muluc, after the thunder and rain, because it was a strong name and it was good to please the water gods. Her name was the same as the day she was born; the Mayans had names for every day. We have Sunday, Monday, Tuesday . . . but they had twenty day names representing different gods, elements, or animals, like rain, wind, or rabbit.

Daykeepers and priests kept track of the calendar, and people could tell the future by tracking the days."

I loved reading my horoscope, so keeping track of the days made sense to me. Despite reason number 40 (mean tour guide), I leaned in closer so I could hear Nando's story and ignore the laughter and talking behind me.

Nando went on. "When Muluc turned fourteen, her parents began to arrange for her marriage to her father's apprentice."

At fourteen? Oh-so popular Fiona's not even allowed to date yet. I imagined my parents trying to find me and my flatter-than-flat chest a husband. I'd end up with someone like that kid in our neighborhood who eats his scabs.

"Who was the apprentice?" Barb asked. "Did she love him?"

Nando closed his eyes and sighed.

"Sorry. No more questions." Barb waved her hands frantically. "Promise."

"Muluc's father was a scribe, which meant that he made books about the gods and kings and priests. He was a powerful man because he could read and most of the kingdom could not."

"The Mayans had books?" Barb asked.

Nando snorted. "Libraries of books, until the Spanish burned them."

"Burned them?" I asked in spite of myself.

He looked right at me. "No more interruptions, or I'll stop."

"Sorry." I tried to sound really sarcastic. "Like I care."

"My story begins on the day called ten Manik. Manik means war and sacrifice. Ten was an unlucky day."

. . .

THE DAY 10 MANIK
War and Sacrifice
Ten was an unlucky number.

Muluc rose from her reed mat when she heard the spider monkeys chattering in the trees. A warm breeze fluttered through the compound, so maybe a storm would finally come today. Her mother slept with her little brother in her arms as Muluc walked barefoot across the cool marble floors, stopping at the doorway of her father's workshop, where she heard the servants beating bark to make paper. Her father was up and working, preparing a screen book honoring the rain gods. The king had ordered a special ceremony and ball game to appease the gods and to bring rain so the corn harvest would not be lost.

Muluc smiled at her father's short hair shooting out of his headband in a tangle. Quills and brushes dripping with paint stuck out of the headband at all angles, making him look like a strange bird. Parrot Nose leaned over him, nodding. Her parents wanted her to marry Parrot Nose because he was one of the king's nephews and might rule someday, but Muluc didn't like his looks—his forehead was too short, he was a little too tall, and his nose looked just like a parrot's beak. He treated her kindly when he bothered to notice her at all, but Muluc figured he'd rather be married to her father. She wasn't ready to be a boring married woman, spending her days weaving and nursing children; she enjoyed her freedom, what little she managed to have.

She tiptoed past the workshop and walked down the steps outside, despite her mother's warning not to leave the compound, because the royal priests had predicted raids from other kingdoms. Muluc thought her mother simply wanted to keep her home to fetch things—like a common servant!

"Muluc! Come back now." Her mother's voice startled her. "You know what I said."

"I was just looking for the monkeys."

Her mother raised an eyebrow.

"Really!" Muluc said.

"Come help me prepare the chocolate for your father."

"And Parrot Nose?"

"You know we don't want you calling him that. It's disrespectful."

After her mother's slave fetched hot water from the cooking hut, Muluc ground the cocoa beans, finally pouring the chocolate and water back and forth from one cup to another until it foamed.

As she served the chocolate, Parrot Nose smiled,

showing off the beautiful jade beads embedded in his teeth. Muluc ran her tongue across her smooth teeth; she couldn't wait until she was old enough to have her teeth jeweled.

Muluc set a bowl of chocolate in front of her father, looking over his shoulder to read the ancient date he'd painted on the bark paper. Most girls didn't read, but Muluc was smart and curious, so her father had allowed her to learn. Parrot Nose didn't seem to mind her reading either; she had to give him credit for that.

When Muluc returned to her mother's rooms, the sun had risen high above the trees. No rain would fall today. Her mother spoke with the blind woman from the market, bartering for flowers to make dye for her cloth and for Father's paints.

The blind woman turned her cloudy eyes toward Muluc. "Ah. Your daughter is growing graceful like a jungle cat."

"Yes. Muluc is almost ready for marriage," her mother said.

"You have a powerful presence," the blind woman said to Muluc. "You possess the thunder in your name."

Her mother laughed. "She is as stubborn as the rain gods have been this growing season."

"She doesn't yet know her strength," the blind woman said.

Muluc backed out of the room. The blind woman made her nervous with her ominous predictions. What did an ugly old woman like her know?

With her mother busy, Muluc ran out of the compound and into the sweltering courtyard. Even the birds had stopped singing as the sun blazed high in the sky, although in the distance she could hear slaves pulling rocks up the side of the king's new temple. Muluc wondered if she would get a new dress to wear to the first temple ceremony—maybe something orange to set off her shiny black hair.

Muluc decided to go swimming in the lagoon. The crocodiles would be hiding in the deep mud to escape the midday heat. She wore plain clothes and tucked her jade pendant beneath her blouse so any guards she encountered wouldn't know she was a scribe's daughter—elites weren't allowed to leave the city boundaries because of the priests' warnings.

Muluc left the white paved roads and found the rough jungle trail to the lagoon. A bright blue bird followed her, squawking and diving down at her.

"Leave me alone."

She brushed the bird away from her head with her hands and walked toward the far side of the lagoon. There weren't as many crocodiles on this side because the common people hunted them for food. The bird followed, still squawking and diving, but she ignored it and watched the water shimmering blue in the sunlight through the green leaves.

Wham! Something knocked Muluc to the ground. A rock cut her cheek. She lay on the ground, stunned, watching her blood drip into the dry dirt. She lifted her head, dizzy and confused, as a man pulled her hands behind her back. Why wasn't he helping her stand? Why wasn't he apologizing for knocking her down? Muluc struggled when the man tied her hands and feet with vines. She screamed for the guards, but the man cupped his rough hand over her mouth and lifted her up, pressing her back against him. Blood pooled in her mouth. Did this man know who her father was? He would be severely punished for treating her roughly, like a commoner! She spit at the man's fishy-smelling hand. He slapped her head so hard that she almost fell down again. Muluc twisted and turned, fighting against his strength. Pivoting, she saw that he had blue streaks painted on his cheeks. He was not from Cobá.

He motioned to another man, then carried Muluc off on his shoulders as if she were a woven sack. Muluc's heartbeat thumped rapidly against the man's stony shoulder, and she kicked at him until he hit her head again. The jungle was full of warriors; soon the air filled with the shouts of war, drums, whistles, and shell trumpets. As she was

carried past the city, Muluc heard screaming, shout-
ing, and wailing. Tears mixed with the blood on her
cheek, stinging.

· · ·

When the bus rattled up to our hotel, Mom and another woman
waved to us from a cluster of plush chairs in the open-air lobby.
I kind of felt bad for her, hanging out in the vomitorium all
day, but I'm sure she took a few minutes for a swim, maybe
ordered a drink by the pool, browsed the various gift shops,
and for sure ate lunch at the buffet place—not in a sandy hut.
And from the looks of it, she made more friends than I did.
Mom walked past the big lobby aquarium—filled with colorful
fish, not scary eels—still chatting with the other woman.

"We can't leave now," Barb said.

"Maybe I'll tell you more tomorrow," Nando said.
"Or not."

"Oh, please. Please." Barb clasped her hands to her chest,
smiled all coy, and batted her eyelashes.

Oh, *por favor!*

"Barb, you little cutie," Talia said as she got off the bus.
"Will you sit by me tomorrow?"

"But Nando—" she said.

"I get it. You're too popular." Talia laughed, tossing her
blue-blond hair, and looked at me like my personality hovered
around a 1.6. Great. My mom *and* my nine-year-old sister make
friends better than I do. I cringed when I thought about what

Fiona's Five would be doing at mini-camp. What if they made special T-shirts like last year? I wouldn't have one—all year long. I thought about how Fiona wouldn't let Grace Williams sit with us at lunch when we were all wearing our mini-camp T-shirts. Every single Tuesday. I glanced at the lobby clock—it was just after four p.m. back home. Did they remember to think of me?

I trudged back to our room feeling small and weak and so tired. Mom walked next to me, not saying anything. Sometimes she knew when to let me be.

Barb bounded ahead of us, her reflection shining in the marble tiles that reminded me of Nando's description of Muluc's house. "I can't wait to tell Dad about all the fish I saw," she said to me. "And about Nando's story. Do you think she escapes?"

"I really don't care." My mouth felt dry and my stomach felt sour. I'd probably contracted some terrible disease from that snorkel mask. Symptoms: fatigue, sore muscles, dehydration, nausea, loneliness, fear, and jealousy.

Mom better reconsider flying home.

CHAPTER FOUR

"Wake up!" Barb rattled around in the dark, stuffing things into her backpack.

"I feel sick." My muscles ached, and my skin burned. Oh, no! I sat up and tried to see if my shoulders glowed in the dark with a cancer-causing sunburn.

Mom opened our adjoining door. "Your dad's still asleep. He's finally keeping everything down, so now he just needs rest." She looked at me. "Where do you get to go today?"

Barb swept her hands wide, as if introducing a circus act. "The ancient city of Tulum."

"I'm not going anywhere with these third-degree burns on my shoulders," I said. "You realize that was reason number twenty-three, don't you?"

"Lighten up, Kat." Mom shook her head. "At least you're having a vacation. Just put more sunscreen on today."

"I wish I'd packed long sleeves." I searched through my suitcase, cursing myself for bringing so many tank tops. "I can't expose myself to any more sunlight."

"Lighten up, Kat." Barb imitated Mom by crossing her arms.

"Reason number twenty-nine," I said.

"What's that?" Barb asked.

"Reason number twenty-nine states that Barb will drive me crazy."

Barb's eyes welled with tears, and she pouted.

"Kat." Mom shot me a stern look before smiling at Barb as if she was the cutest kitten in the litter. "I've heard those ruins are beautiful, sweetheart." She glanced back at her own room, where Dad moaned for a drink of water. "I hope tomorrow we'll get out of here."

"And fly home?" I asked.

"You'd really rather be home, cooped up at Fiona's house, watching videos you've already seen?" Mom asked.

"It's a lot more than that, though I don't expect you to ever understand."

"Sometimes I don't know why we bother," Mom said. "You're only interested in two-star movies and nail polish. I give up."

"Don't be sad, sweet little Mommy." Barb hugged her. "I'm learning so much that I want to stay here forever."

Oh, yeah. Reason number 29.

The lobby was full of tourists with backpacks and whining kids waiting for buses. Talia waited too, wearing the shorts from Abercrombie that Fiona said would make me look "oh-so height-challenged." The Bronze Sun Goddess leaned against the exchange desk getting pesos; the guy helping her smiled so big it looked like his face would break.

"Hey, Barb!" Talia flipped her blue hair. "You were totally

right about the fruit at breakfast. I think it *is* better on the right side of the buffet."

"We could do a taste test tomorrow!" Barb said.

"I love it. You're such a little scientist!"

Barb and Talia planned out three days' worth of fruit testing while I stood by myself like a dorky loser. Talia hardly even looked at me, and I felt so stupid wearing my dumb old hiking shorts. I moped around the lobby, miserable about missing Mini-camp Makeover Morning followed by glamour-shot photos for the scrapbook, not to mention shopping and lunch downtown. I got nervous just thinking about the scrapbook. I'd be completely absent—like a missing person. Like I didn't even exist. I glanced over at the gift shop. If I sent more postcards, Fiona would have to include them in the scrapbook, right? So what if that strategy didn't work for Grace Williams? She sent tons of e-mails for the scrapbook, but Fiona deleted them because "electronic communication is oh-so impersonal." So why does she take it oh-so personally if we don't answer one of the online quizzes she forwards? I'd thought about checking my e-mail in the hotel business center, but it seemed kind of sad and pathetic to waste pool and beach time hanging out with a bunch of workaholic dads. Besides, postcards were better, right?

Just then the bus chug-chug-rattled up. Barb sat up front, near where Nando would sit, even though Talia begged her to sit in the back with the group. No one asked me to sit in the back with the group. New reason, number 41: mean teen tourists. I watched as Talia sat in front of the cheerleaders, who were too busy talking to notice her. Ha! I saw that the Bronze Sun Goddess had chosen: Dante the Hunky Blond sat next to her. Luc stared out the window in the seat behind them. Poor guy (and a 10 too). If only I had more to offer. I sat in the seat behind Barb, two rows behind the driver, trying not to look quite so immature.

A bigger tourist bus loaded passengers in front of us, so Alfredo stood up and started talking. *"Buenos días."*

"Buenos días," everyone shouted.

"Hey, you expert Spanish speakers, eh?" People laughed. Alfredo was pretty cute with his shaggy hair and big smile. Yup, a solid 9.

"Today we go to the ancient ruins of Tulum. Spanish explorers saw this city from the sea and sailed past. The city looked so—how you say?"

"Formidable?" I answered, caring only a little that I looked like a total teacher's pet. I'd been flipping through Barb's Mayan book last night for a picture of Cobá, and I came across a drawing of what Tulum would have looked like—all busy and full of boats and people. The caption called it too formidable for the Spanish, or something. I'm not *really* that "oh-so fact remembering" as Fiona says.

"Formidable." Alfredo flashed a smile my way and pushed his hair away from his face. "The city was trading place. Big canoes from all over Mexico landed on the beach. A wall surrounded the city. You can still see the wall today."

The bus groaned and lurched when Alfredo turned the key. I imagined getting stranded on some lonely road, being attacked by bandits and sold into slavery, although that might be a better fate than missing mini-camp.

We picked Nando up at the same spot along the road. He hadn't even sat down before Barb started nagging him with questions. "Tell us about the girl. Does she survive? Do they hurt her baby brother? Where are they taking her?"

Nando ignored her.

"Tell us the stooooory." Barb drew out the word "story" so it had about a million syllables. "Pleeese."

I leaned forward, tapping Barb on the arm. "Don't make him mad." I glanced at Nando, hunched down low in his seat like a jaguar waiting to pounce. "Quit bugging him."

"I never promised to finish the story." Nando looked out the window. "Maybe I don't feel like wasting it on tourists."

"I know! I'll tell you a story first." Barb ignored my warning punch in the shoulder and slid across the aisle to Nando's seat. I imagined Mom crying her eyes out when I told her about Barb being strangled by a dangerous stranger on the stupid teen tour, but she couldn't say that I hadn't warned her.

Barb went on and on about the big mountains in Utah and our cats Marvin and Harvey, her room with pink butterflies on the wallpaper, how she wished we had a dog like her friend Sophie, how math was her favorite subject in school but she was also a good reader like her friend Emma. Blah blah blah. I couldn't tell if Nando was listening or not, but he'd score major points at mini-camp for sweetness. Personally, I wanted to strangle her.

"So, where we pick you up, where does that road go? Fancy pyramids?" asked Barb.

"No. Just a small village," Nando said.

"Why can't the bus go to your house? My school bus goes right to my house. Well, really it's the next house over, but—"

"Barb." Why did she keep ignoring me? I shifted forward on the seat to avoid a patch of scratchy duct tape.

"You can only get to my village by foot or horseback." Nando stared straight ahead. Why couldn't Barb buy a clue?

"Horses! You have horses? That's so cool. I'd love to ride a horse everywhere."

Nando scoffed. "No, you'd rather have your smooth roads and fancy cars. Believe me."

"How far is it?" Barb wouldn't shut up.

"Three kilometers or so."

Barb gasped. "Three miles!"

"It's more like two miles." I couldn't help myself. After all, I'd gotten an A in honors math. Nando glanced back at me, but I couldn't read his expression.

"Do you have grocery stores and stuff in your village? We have a Dan's—that's a grocery store—really close, but sometimes my mom goes to Wild Oats."

"Rich American *turistas*." Nando shook his head. "No. We grow all our own food. Fruits, vegetables, chickens, pigs."

"That's so cool. My mom wouldn't let me grow a garden this summer; she said we were traveling too much," Barb said. "What about electricity?"

"My cousin has a generator, but most of us don't have any."

"Do you have a TV?" Barb asked. Was she even thinking? Or was her mouth on shuffle? Random thought. Random thought. Random thought.

"If there's no electricity, you wouldn't have a TV." I moved to the seat behind Nando and Barb to avoid all that duct tape, plus I'd be close enough to cover Barb's mouth with my hand.

"Oh, yeah."

"My cousin uses his generator to watch TV," Nando said. "We're not just ignorant peasants." He looked at me.

"Hey, won't we get to see your house," Barb asked, "when we go to your sister's party?"

Nando glanced back at me again. "I guess." He sounded as thrilled about it as I did.

Hopefully, we could just skip that whole thing.

The bus pulled up to a row of shops selling sombreros, pottery, silver — a mall without walls or doors.

Alfredo stood up. "Welcome to Tulum," he said. "We take tram to ruins, have tour, eat picnic lunch — lots of iguanas, very tasty." No one laughed. "Joke, joke," he said. "We have Mexican picnic — tortillas, fruit, good stuff."

We climbed off the bus and headed down a sandy road toward the tram. Monique and Dante held hands. The cheerleaders actually turned cartwheels. Please! Barb kept stopping to look at big piles of stones.

"Let's go," I said.

"Maybe some secret treasure is buried under one of these mounds."

"That is just an old rock wall," Nando said, coming up behind us.

Soon we came to a clearing, where we waited for the tram with a crowd of people.

Barb pouted. "This is too much like Disneyland," she said. "How can I find treasure if everything has already been explored?"

"There are still many treasures to find," Nando said. "Pirates hid gold on this coast, and some ships sank. There's a beach near here where jewels from an old pirate ship still wash up on the shore after storms."

"Really?" Barb tilted her curly little head. "There was a storm two days ago." She got that look. "Oh, I bet there's some new treasure just waiting for me!"

"Barb, give it up," I said as we slid into our seats on the tram. While Barb rambled about gold coins, I stared out at the bushes and trees crowding the side of the road like pushy tourists. A salty-scented breeze rattled the palm fronds, and I felt too far from home. I sucked in a breath of humid air, wishing I were back in dry—and, yeah, brown—Utah with my friends.

The tram stopped, and we walked through a gap in the wall into the ancient city that had been built on a bluff above the Caribbean. Beyond the sun-bleached stone buildings, the aqua-colored water sparkled all the way to the horizon. Pausing by a small stone building at the entrance, the guide explained that the rulers, priests, and craftsmen had lived within the city walls while the lower classes lived without the protection of walls. Sounded a lot like junior high: being one of Fiona's Five was like having a protective wall. The guide pointed out the castles for the elite as we walked over to a platform with a thatched roof, where a craftsman had lived.

While we stood in the shade, he told us the story of ten shipwrecked Spaniards who were captured when they landed on the coast near the city. Most of the men were killed immediately in a sacrificial ceremony, and the meat of their bodies was served to the people in a cannibalistic feast. C.C. and Jessie squealed in disgust. I knew these people were dangerous. Why didn't Mom believe me? Mental note—add reason number 42: cannibalism.

"Five of the men were too skinny—like supermodels, eh?" The guide smiled as we laughed. "They were kept in a cage to fatten up."

I glanced around to see which of us would be served in a feast. My hormone deficiency might have saved me, but Monique would have made a tasty meal. I watched her wiggle her perfectly painted toes. No—she would've been crowned queen.

"The prisoners escaped and ran to another Lord, who kept them alive as slaves," the guide said. Maybe Fiona would allow me to survive missing mini-camp if I carried her books, did her homework, folded her laundry, or cleaned her room (wait . . . I did that once). Grace Williams hadn't thought of that! She once brought cookies to share during lunch, but Fiona called them "oh-so store-bought" and ignored her.

The guide continued. "One, Gonzalo de Guerrero, pierced his nose, lips, and ears and tattooed his hands. He married a Mayan woman and had many children. When the Spanish arrived, he refused to leave with them."

That's what Maya-obsessed Barb would do. Or was that what *I* was doing—trying so hard to fit in? I touched my short hair, which Fiona had told me to cut in a layered bob because it would be "oh-so matching" if we all had the same hairstyle. I had liked my long hair, but I cut it anyway to belong to the group.

"De Guerrero stayed with the Mayans and helped them to fight against the Spaniards. The other man, Gerónimo de Aguilar, helped Cortés conquer the Aztecs and Mayans by acting as an interpreter." The guide stopped and looked around at each of us before Barb broke the silence and asked about pirate treasure.

Staying with the group was a good thing, right? But then I felt confused. Which guy stayed with his group? The Spanish guy who betrayed the Mayans? Or the guy who betrayed the Spanish and lived Mayan?

We walked over bumpy limestone to the castle, which was built near the edge of the water, like a movie star's mansion. The guide talked about how the buildings were designed to show the cycles of the sun and Venus. Turns out the Mayans were pretty good at math too. Barb peered over the cliff at the narrow beach below while I watched a pair of iguanas chase each other over the rocks into a group of stunted palms. When I looked back, Barb was gone.

"Do you see my sister?" I asked the English girls, Gemma and Anna.

Gemma pointed to the cliff. "I think she might have gone exploring."

Way, way down, Barb jumped off a large gray rock onto the sand and picked up something.

"Barb!" I yelled. "Come back!"

Rock outcroppings surrounded the beach. Barb reached up to the big boulder and tried to pull herself up, looking so tiny as she threw her hands in the air. She shrieked as a wave curled around her ankles.

I started down the steep path, thinking Barb must be part mountain goat to get down this thing. I slipped in a sandy section, scraping my hand on a sharp rock. Finally I got down near the beach and jumped off the huge boulder.

Barb held up a bottle cap. "It glittered like gold from up there."

"Thousands of people walk through here every day," I said. "You're not going to find any treasure. You'd be lucky to find a seashell or an interesting rock."

I walked over to the big rock. "Let me give you a boost." I shoved her onto its stony surface, but I couldn't get back up: too short. A big wave splashed around the cuffs of my shorts. I reached with my hand and tried to find a hold for my foot, but my legs were too stubby. I plopped back on the sand just in time to be soaked by another wave. I really was going to be killed in a rip tide! And that wasn't even *on* my list of reasons.

Dante ran down the path, jumped onto the sand, cupped his hand, and nodded to me. I put my soggy shoe in his hands and gripped the rock.

"Thanks so much," I said.

People up above cheered, even the flower-shirted tourists. Several snapped photos. Great. I'd be the loser tourist in some stranger's scrapbook.

I scrambled up the path as quick as I could, with Dante following right behind, getting a great view of my wet butt. At least I had something exciting, not to mention true, to put in my next postcard to Fiona: Rescued by Hunky Blond Belgian. I didn't have to say it was because of my silly, treasure-seeking sister and my excessively short stature.

"Strong legs," Dante said before racing up the last few feet to meet up with Monique. I totally blushed, lost my balance, and slipped, getting sand all over my wet shirt.

Alfredo set up the picnic lunch in the field where the craftsmen had lived. Everyone snacked on fruit while he talked about the big trading canoes landing between the cliffs on the wide beach that came right into the city. Why hadn't Barb spotted gold twinkling on that actually accessible beach? I brushed more sand off my drying shirt.

"Nice going, wet one," Talia said to me before turning to Barb. "You okay, cutie? I would've rescued you."

Barb started telling Talia about the sunken pirate treasure, so I walked toward the water, pulled off my wet shoes, and waded in the surf to a flat rock. I took out my journal and added new reasons to my list. Number 43: beaches where you can get stranded and nearly killed; number 44: being the loser tourist in some stranger's scrapbook. Next to a drawing I'd started of Muluc, I quickly sketched a comical tourist photo of myself, but then Nando walked toward me, so I stashed the journal back in my knapsack.

"Have a tortilla," he said. "My mother made them."

"I'm not hungry." My stomach rumbled, but I wasn't going

to let Nando be nice because he pitied me. New reason, number 45: inspiring pity from even the meanest (see number 40) tour guide.

Nando glanced at my stomach. "Try it."

I dangled my feet in the water, letting an incoming wave splash my legs.

"Okay." I bit into the soft, fresh tortilla. "This is actually pretty good." I spent only a fraction of a second worrying that Nando was trying to poison me, and then I devoured the rest of it. Nando handed me another one.

"*Mi mamá* makes the best," he said.

Barb ran over to us with a stack of tortillas and some fruit. She leaned forward. "Tell us what happens to Muluc."

• • •

THE DAY 11 LAMAT
Dragon, Sign of the Planet Venus—the Great Star

Muluc and the other prisoners from Cobá walked all night through the jungle. The animal and spirit sounds frightened Muluc as much as her captors did. When someone fell or slowed down, the warriors whipped them with vine rope. As she began to feel weak, her hands still tied with vines, Muluc concentrated on placing one foot in front of the other and watching her step. She'd seen a girl ahead of her fall, bloodying her whole face and knocking out her front teeth.

"Leave her," a warrior said, "She's no good now—the gods won't want her, and neither will the Lords."

Muluc had looked back at the girl, obviously a commoner. The girl's pitiful whimpers made the hairs on Muluc's arms stand up straight, but she walked on, holding her head high, wondering how the warriors would treat a member of the elite class. Should she tell them? They would likely release her.

In the morning, sun filtered down through the leaves, drying the blood on Muluc's cheek until it felt tight and itchy. Above, a howler monkey bounced on a branch, waiting for its mate to swing over from another tree. Yesterday she had felt as free as one of them, Muluc thought, blinking away burning tears.

Soon the group left the thick grove of trees and found themselves on a vast wasteland of sand. Muluc stumbled, falling once, but scrambled to her feet before anyone noticed. Some of the smaller children had fallen and lay bawling.

Muluc recognized a boy she'd seen fishing with his father in the lagoon. He worked his hands up and down to free them from the vines. Moments later she saw him sprint away from the group. One of the warriors ran after him but gave up after a brief chase. Muluc wished she had the spirit and strength to escape, but she wouldn't be able to find her way back anyway.

At the edge of the sand, Muluc saw the biggest water she had ever seen: it roared toward the shore, lashing out at the sand, retreating, and lashing out again. She did not walk any closer. Others stopped behind her, and children cried out. The warriors laughed and shoved the people toward crudely built cages near the water.

"Girls here," said a warrior with blue streaks painted on his cheeks. "Men who can work, here. Keep the elite separate."

Muluc started to announce her elite status, but she stopped as the man with blue streaks grabbed her bound wrists and looked at her. "You're attractive for a commoner," he said. "With the right clothes you'd almost make a princess." Muluc flushed hot with shame under his leering gaze. From behind, someone shoved her shoulder.

"Get in the cage," a voice said. Muluc turned and saw a tall man with a tattoo of a feathered snake wrapped around his neck. His long hair, tied up on top of his head, was studded with jewels. A rod of jade pierced his nose, and he wore a loincloth with an embroidered serpent climbing the World Tree. Muluc stumbled in the sand and staggered into the cage before he could touch her again.

The sun left the sky to return to the Otherworld,

and the stars sparkled brightly. Muluc huddled with the other girls as a breeze cooled the sand and her bare arms.

"I'm hungry," a small girl said.

"Quiet," another whispered.

Muluc's stomach rumbled with hunger. At last she slept.

All night the blue jay squawked at her in her dreams. Sometimes the bird spoke to her in her mother's voice: "You disobeyed me. You disobeyed the king." Other times it pecked her scalp until she bled. "Listen. Listen. Don't ignore me," it screeched.

• • •

THE DAY 12 MULUC
Water, Thunder, and Jade

The door opened, waking Muluc as a skinny girl with long, matted hair and tattered clothes entered the cage. Muluc had never seen such a girl at Cobá—so poor-looking, bony, and unclean. The girl carried a gourd and handed it to each of the captives, letting them drink for a moment. Muluc's mouth watered just thinking about the rich taste of chocolate. She drank a big gulp, choking on the cold, watery gruel made from the coarsest corn-meal—the kind saved for pigs! She made an effort to swallow the gritty, bland liquid without gagging.

The sun rose from the Otherworld, warming the cold sand. Soon flies buzzed around the cage. Several of the girls had wet themselves, and the air reeked. Muluc walked to the corner, squatted, and peed, trying not to get her clothes wet. She wanted to weep at such humiliation, but didn't dare draw attention to herself.

The warriors divided the men and boys into groups, putting them into large canoes, bigger than any the fishermen had on the lakes of Cobá. Among the men she noticed a few with royal markings—one looked like Parrot Nose's brother! Three men wearing royal capes kneeled on the sand. The warriors painted them with black and white stripes, whipping them with thorny vines when they didn't cooperate. Muluc felt her heart beat fast. Had the warriors made it into the city, to the royal compound, to her father's compound? She searched the faces of the captives for her family. Most of the captives looked like commoners: strong-bodied men, young boys, and girls. No elders. The warrior with the snake tattoo came over to Muluc's cage, but she avoided his eyes; acting common might keep her safe.

"Come," he said, pulling girls up by their wrists. "Dunk them in the sea," he said to the boy with him. "They stink."

The boy led the girls into the angry water; they screamed as the foamy waves splashed over their bodies, almost knocking them over. The boy grabbed Muluc.

"I'm not dirty." She pushed the boy away, so he chose a younger girl who had a yellow stain on her skirt.

The warrior with the snake ordered the girls placed in his canoe. Squeezing into the tight spaces between jars and baskets, the girls sat down on the rough wooden bottom. Many whimpered with fear.

"Don't touch anything," Snake said. "It's all more valuable than any of you."

Muluc huddled low next to a large basket that smelled sweet, like the incense her mother burned at the family altar. She buried her face in her hands and cried, just like the common girls with urine-soaked clothes.

When the sun burned high above them, the men shoved the canoes into the rolling waves. Muluc watched the shore grow distant, but the rhythm of the boat rocking in the water and the heat of the sun soon put her to sleep. She dreamed of nothing.

"Wake up." Snake jabbed Muluc with his foot. "Here."

He placed a piece of coconut in her mouth, then gave her a sip of water from a gourd. The coconut tasted sweet, like home. Snake studied Muluc, handing her a second chunk of coconut.

"You have a long forehead for a commoner," he said. "Pretty stone in your lip too."

Muluc looked down.

"They found you outside the city?" Snake asked.

"Yes," Muluc said.

"You're certainly dressed like a commoner." Snake paused. "I should get a good price for a girl like you anyway." As Snake moved away, Muluc shivered despite the warm sun.

Fear darkened Muluc's mood as clouds darkened the sky. Had they entered the Otherworld? She feared they were taking her to the edge of the world to dump her as a sacrifice to the gods. With the sharp end of the vine that bound her hands, she pierced her lip and let the blood drip onto the floor of the canoe as an offering. She prayed to the water gods that she would survive and find her family again.

That night, the canoe tossed in the dark sea. Water splashed over the sides, soaking the captive girls. Some cried, others screamed. One girl stood and tried to jump out, but Snake tied her down.

"Stupid girl," he hissed, pressing his foot into her back.

Muluc's mouth ached with thirst, so she licked the water droplets off her arm. Salt! The fresh cut on her lip stung as she hunkered down to avoid the cold spray. A bolt of lightning lit the sky in a brilliant flash. Girls shrieked.

"The gods are already pleased with us," Snake said.

Muluc knew the gods were angry. Lightning struck the sea again and again as the thunder gods called her name. If she survived this night, she could be strong. A wave washed over her, tipping the canoe at an angle. A small girl stood up, screaming for her mother.

"Sit down!" Snake yelled.

But the girl wouldn't listen, and the next big wave knocked her into the sea. The other girls sat still, stunned. Muluc tried to pierce her lip again to make an offering to the thunder gods, but the canoe shook and listed so that she could barely hang on. Again the boat tipped, and another girl tumbled into the water.

"Untie their hands," Snake said. "Or the gods will take them all."

The boy stumbled between the baskets to reach the girls. With an obsidian knife he slit Muluc's vines; quickly, as the boat shuddered in the storm, she grasped the nearest rope, knowing that Snake would have fastened his cargo so that nothing could shake it loose.

Waves crashed over the canoe as it rolled through the swells. Soon rain poured down. Muluc held tight as the boat tilted upward and rain beat at her face like tears from the gods. Over and over she repeated her prayers.

The storm ceased as the morning light seeped into the sky, turning it the delicate hues of pink, ripe melon. When Muluc released her grip on the rope, her hand cramped like an eagle's claw. She rubbed her knuckles and eased her fingers apart: a rope burn slithered across her palm like a red snake.

Muluc looked around and noticed that several baskets had disappeared and clay pots had broken. Many more girls had been lost. Snake stood at the front of the canoe staring into the water.

"There," he said to the boy. "See it?"

The boy jabbed at the water with a long spear.

"Roll it first, then spear it," Snake said.

The boy stabbed the water with more force and pulled up a giant turtle.

"Aha!" Snake laughed. "This will make up for some of my losses." He took the turtle off the spear and rubbed his hand over its multicolored shell. Muluc had never seen such a massive turtle in the lakes of Cobá. Slitting the turtle with his knife, Snake poured the entrails into a clay jar before cutting a bit of meat off the carcass.

"Mmm." Snake licked his lips and noticed Muluc staring. "You want a taste, pretty girl?"

Muluc held out her hand; Snake walked over, looking down at her palm.

"You've got a strong spirit," he said. "You held on tight." He squeezed the meat so that juices ran along the red snake on her palm. "Turtle oil will take out the sting."

Snake dropped the meat onto Muluc's palm. Her stomach rumbled with so much hunger that she would eat almost anything, and she eagerly chewed the rubbery, wet glob.

The sun rose, drying Muluc's clothes and hair; salt crystals crusted her skin like scales. Not caring about proper manners, she licked her arm; the salt made the turtle meat taste better.

A flock of big white birds flew low near the canoe—one dipped into the water, scooping up a fish in its stretchy beak. Muluc looked out at the calm, sparkling sea. In the distance, she saw a shimmer of green.

CHAPTER FIVE

Beach day! Glorious beach day. No tour activities. No Nando rolling his eyes at me. No teens ignoring me. No potential for embarrassment. Dad was still feeling a little weak, so he and Mom decided to hang out at the beach. I didn't care about jellyfish or even sharks, but I did get up early to reserve a spot under a thatched umbrella so I could avoid those cancer rays. I wrote a postcard:

• • •

Hi! Yesterday I went to this beautiful Mayan castle on the Caribbean—see front.
The guys are so sweet. Dante even rescued me from a big wave.
He's a 10++. Tonight we're going clubbing at the pier in Playa.
You won't recognize me with my tan.
Love 4ever, Kat
P.S. Remember, remember, remember!!!!

• • •

Five postcards in four days.

"What are you writing about?" Barb asked.

I hid the postcard in my journal.

"Nothing. Just about yesterday."

"About how we couldn't get up from that beach?"

"Sure," I said.

"You really should tell them about Nando's story." Barb tapped her travel journal. "I'm trying to write it all down."

"You're such a goon," I said.

"Am not."

"Are too."

"Admit it," Barb said. "You like the story."

"It's okay. Not really my thing." I put my sunglasses on and laid back. Truth? I loved the story, even if I still thought Nando was a mean, and possibly dangerous, kidnapper. I kept thinking about Muluc. What would I do in her situation? I wondered if I could stay strong. Or would I be freaking out like the girls on the boat? I would've drowned in the ocean yesterday if someone hadn't rescued me. Was I good at anything? I made a list of my qualities: smart, funny sometimes, nice eyes, okay artist. Short, short, and short. Prepubescent. People took one look at me and treated me like a child. Fiona and the gang joked about my height too. I usually just laughed along with them, even when it really hurt.

Yesterday on the way back from Tulum, Talia made some dumb joke that I'd tried to sacrifice myself to the gods when I rescued Barb. Everyone laughed except the Bronze Sun Goddess and Dante, who were too busy cuddling. And Nando—he stared out the window in his usual tour bus mode.

"Are you sure you're really thirteen?" she asked. "You're so short and, you know—" She looked down at my flat chest. Then she asked Barb to come sit with her. The traitor agreed! I sat in the seat behind Nando, feeling like the world's biggest loser.

"You know, some of the best cheerleaders are short," Jessie said a few minutes later, as if she'd been contemplating my short stature the whole time.

"Totally," said C.C. "El Dorado, our major rival, has this Mexican girl who is sooo tiny, but can she fly."

"We need someone like that," Jessie said.

"You have a lot of Mexicans where you live?" Talia asked.

"I'm from Texas. What do you think?"

Josh leaned forward. "Are they all illegal?"

"Some, probably." C.C. shrugged.

"My dad says illegal immigrants are ruining the country," Josh said.

"People complain about that in Texas."

"California too," Jessie said.

"They come here not speaking English and expect us to pay for them."

What were they saying? Right in front of Nando and Alfredo. I mean it's not like I really care or anything, but it's rude. I'd never stand in front of the remedial kids and say they were ruining our school's test scores. Did Nando hear them? I watched him squeeze his eyes shut and roll his hands into fists.

I leaned over. "How come you don't say anything?"

He didn't look at me. "I'll get fired."

"But you don't even seem to like this job."

"My family needs the money." Nando looked down at his balled-up hands.

"I thought you grew everything you needed—that's what you said on the bus this morning. Fruits? Vegetables? Chickens?"

Nando had looked out the window at a hotel emerging from the jungle. "It's not enough anymore."

Everyone laughed at some joke Talia told about Mexicans changing a light bulb. When I glared at her, she stuck her tongue out at me. So mature. Barb bounced on the seat next to her. Oblivious. Who's the one trying too hard to fit in? That joke was *so* rude! Talia smirked at me.

"Why don't *you* say anything to her?" Nando said. Why did he have to turn around right at that moment?

I shrugged. I wasn't about to tell him that I never said anything to anyone who teased me. I just went along with it like it was my joke too. I wanted everyone to like me, even stupid Talia.

"You don't have anything to lose by standing up for yourself," Nando said. "But you can lose yourself by trying to please everyone."

I snorted and looked out the window. What did he know? He wasn't exactly standing up for himself, and he didn't know anything about clinging to a popular group of friends by the thinnest thread.

• • •

I perched on the edge of my beach chair, squishing my feet into the sand, and read my postcard again. Full of lies to make me look good—make them like me. So stupid! My parents would never let me go clubbing in a foreign country; I couldn't even go to the movies on a Friday night. Fiona and the Five would know it too. Why was I trying so hard? I imagined what they'd be doing at mini-camp. Talking about everyone. Talking about me: my clothes, my hair, my height, my grades, and my personality flaws. Just like we all slammed Grace Williams last summer. I felt nervous just thinking about it. And then I remembered how Fiona decided we should all switch out of choir and take the dance elective instead. She didn't tell Grace Williams until it was too late and the class was full. I felt all panicky. I jumped up and ran into the waves to wash the feeling off me.

The water felt so good, so warm. I floated with my eyes closed, bobbing with the swells. Just me and the blue-green Caribbean. I flipped over and swam underwater. When I stood up, I saw the Bronze Sun Goddess swimming with another blond. Maybe her brother?

She saw me and waved.

"*Bonjour,* Kat," she said with her fantastic accent.

"Hi, Monique."

"Nice water," she said. "Warm." She stood up.

I was looking at her breasts. Naked, topless breasts. Tan Naked Topless Breasts. Big Tan Naked Topless Breasts!

Omigosh, omigosh, I screamed inside my head, but I couldn't say anything.

Monique laughed.

"You're so cute," she said. "See you later, crocodile."

Monique flipped, dunking under the water, and I headed back to the beach as if a shark were after me. I needed a cold drink. My face flamed. Can you really die from embarrassment? On the way in, I noticed all kinds of women splashing around topless—big and saggy, small and perky, old and wrinkly, but none so perfect as what the Bronze Sun Goddess sported. Why did my parents have to book a hotel with a nude beach? New reason, number 46: nude beach at hotel!

After getting my drink, I rubbed an ice cube on my cheeks.

When I got back to the umbrella, Dad laughed. "You shot out of there like a bullet."

"What?"

"You acted like you'd never seen breasts before," he said.

"She's never seen such big ones," Barb said.

"That's not funny." I dropped a piece of ice down her bathing suit. "What would you know anyway, you little traitor?"

"Oooooh," she squealed, wiggling to shake the ice out. "But your face got so red, it glowed." She laughed. "We could see it all the way over here."

"In Europe, women swim topless all the time," Mom said. "It's the custom."

I rolled my eyes. "Thanks for the geography lesson, but we're not *in* Europe."

"I think it's a great idea." Dad laughed and raised his eyebrows at Mom. "I think you should go European," he said.

"I just might," she said. "I just might."

"Don't you even—" I gasped.

They laughed so hard that Mom choked and spit out her drink. Real classy, Mom.

"I'm glad I'm going on the tour tomorrow," I said.

CHAPTER SIX

The bus came early to drive us three hours through the jungle to the ruins at Chichén Itzá. Mom and Dad were taking it easy for one more day, and I don't even want to think about what that means. Really, their behavior had been disgusting—public kissing, snuggling, all kinds of jokes. If I came back and found my mom topless on the beach, I'd check into a different hotel.

Barb pestered Nando as soon as we picked him up. "What happens next? Tell me, tell me, *tell* me."

"I don't know if I should tell you now or wait until we get there. Or maybe on the way back." He smiled, actually smiled, a big, beautiful smile: a 10 all the way. He turned to me. "What do you think, Kat?"

I totally blushed. Of course Talia was looking right at me. She leaned forward and whispered something to Jessie and C.C. They all laughed, and I knew I was going to be in for it—all day long.

"I don't care," I said. "Whenever."

Nando looked at me like I should say something, but I slumped down in my seat. Someone had scratched a swear-word into the vinyl that pretty much described how I felt.

"Say something." Nando peered down at me. "Be brave like the jaguar in your name."

"I will when you do." What did his name mean? He was probably named after some thorny plant that gave you a rash if you simply looked at it.

"Kat, your face is all red," Barb said.

"Thanks for noticing, *Babs*." Oooh, she hated that nickname.

"You have to be nice to me. Dad said."

"Whatever." Maybe I could find a way to sacrifice her to the gods.

The bus had turned off the main highway and rattled along a narrow road that was thick with trees and bushes in every shade of green. Thinking of my huge box of pastels, I named the colors: cadmium, emerald, olive . . . a patch of cinnabar green. Hot air blew through the windows. Every time I shifted my weight, my sweaty thighs stuck to the seat. And the smell of exhaust made me a little nauseous. The girls in back squealed every time a truck or bus passed, nearly knocking us off the road. I opened my journal to add a new reason, number 47: crazy bus drivers.

"He's driving like we're on the autobahn," Luc said.

Alfredo slammed on the brakes as a truck cut us off. I sat up and gripped Nando's seat in front of me. How many tourists get killed in car accidents? And we didn't even have seat belts. I tried to do some relaxing breathing while I searched out the window for vines like the ones in Muluc's story. I spotted some! Dark leaf green, winding up a pale tree trunk. But then the bus sped up again.

We finally slowed down a bit as we passed a small village of round stick huts with thatched roofs, built close to the road. None had doors, and in some you could see people swinging in hammocks. Sometimes they waved. The bus stopped in front of a small hut with a rock wall surrounding a lush garden with fruit trees.

"Mi bonita," Alfredo called out. A woman in a white dress with red flowers embroidered at the neck and along the bottom walked out of the hut, smiled, and waved.

"Who's that?" Barb asked.

"Alfredo's girlfriend," Nando said. "You will meet her at my sister's *quinceañera.*"

"I can't wait." Barb sighed. "She's so pretty!"

The girl *was* gorgeous. Did Nando have a beautiful girlfriend in a white dress somewhere? Why did I even care? I liked Zach B. with his spiky hair and sense of humor, although he didn't quite match Dante or Luc in the body department. And he wasn't nearly as smart as Nando. I reminded myself of Fiona, always comparing, ranking, rating, and assigning numbers to everyone, for everything.

Alfredo's girlfriend watched, waving as the bus pulled away. All of us on the bus turned around to see her as we drove on.

Talia singsonged, "Alfredo has a girlfriend."

Alfredo took his hands off the steering wheel, put them over his heart, and pretended to swoon. *"Mi amor,"* he said. *"Quien nunca amó y nunca fue amado jamás nació."*

"What does that mean?" Barb asked.

"He who never loved and never was loved was never born," Nando said.

Great—another thing to worry about. Love. Would anyone ever feel that way about me? Zach B. once lent me a pencil in third period, but that probably doesn't count. Fiona had said it was "oh-so ordinary," and nothing like the time Ian Pearl lent her a piece of notebook paper. I sat there fretting about Zach B., not realizing that my hand rested near Nando's neck.

"So, Kat?" Talia called out. "Who's your boyfriend? Is it—"

As girly giggles bubbled throughout the bus, I scrunched down in my seat, got out my journal, and penciled a rough drawing of Muluc riding out the storm.

We drove fast for another stretch and then slowed through a village. Children stared as the bus passed; a skinny dog lay sleeping in the road and almost didn't get out of the way, so Alfredo had to stop. Life seemed so slow out here.

Too slow. All that giggling. I swear I kept hearing my name. Oh, how I just wanted to get this day over with! I pressed my journal to my chest as we passed a small white cement-block building with Spanish words written all over the outside. A sign advertised COLD COCA COLA. Just when it seemed like we were traveling through some ancient period in time, something like that Coke sign would pop up and remind me of home. Would things even be any better at home? Or would I just exchange Talia for Fiona? I shoved my journal into my backpack. My drawings were stupid anyway.

We passed another small building. In the dirt yard, children dressed in blue shorts and white shirts ran around playing soccer.

"What's that?" Barb asked.

"School," Nando said.

Barb crinkled her nose. "It's so small."

"It's a small village." Nando looked back to watch the kids as the bus sped up again. "I went to a school like that."

"Shouldn't you still be in school?" I flew up from my seat as the bus hit a bump in the road. My fingers brushed Nando's shoulder as I grabbed the back of his seat, but I quickly put them in my lap. But not before Talia made some comment about me and *amor*.

"I had to drop out," he said. "To help my family."

"My dad says we have to go to college," Barb said. "That's like going to school forever." She frowned. "I'd rather go exploring all day like you."

Nando's jaw tightened, so I gave Barb a warning look, but she ignored me as usual.

"You should be a teacher," she said. "You'd be really good at it. I'm learning so much from your story." She clapped her hands together. "Tell us more now, please?"

Nando sighed long and sad. "Where did we leave off?"

"Who cares?" I looked out the window at a tree bursting with orange blossoms—it was pretty, but it totally looked out of place in the mass of green plants. Just like me. Minus the pretty part. "It's just a dumb story, Barb," I said, loud enough for Talia to hear. Maybe she'd shut up about all the boyfriend stuff.

I glanced at Nando, ignoring the hurt look in his dark eyes, and stared back out the window. The orange tree was gone, and the rest of the jungle conformed to green, green, green.

"Don't listen to her. She's just being hormonal. Mom says."

I kicked the seat hard. "Shut up, Barb!"

Nando narrowed his eyes at me.

"Please, Nando. *Por favor.*" Barb actually put her hands on his cheeks and moved his face to look at her. "Muluc had just seen a shimmer of green," she said. "It has to be an island, right? Is it Cozumel? My mom and dad might go there and—"

"No." Nando took a deep breath, squaring his shoulders, and said, "It's just a small island on the Gulf side of the Yucatán. Not a tourist place."

"What's it called?"

"Isla Cerritos."

"Ooh! That sounds so pretty. If I get that stuffed turtle at the gift shop, I'm going to name it Cerritos. Okay, tell the story."

Nando leaned back in his seat with his shoulders slumped. "It was the day called Eb."

• • •

THE DAY 2 EB
Rain and Storms

White clouds fluttered across the sky as Muluc's canoe landed on an island just off the shore of the peninsula. A flock of long-legged birds flew over the boat in a rush of pink. What strange land had she entered? Canoes lined the beach like big, lazy crocodiles, and crude thatched huts crowded to-gether. In front of one hut, which was piled high with baskets of fluffy white cotton, two men ar-gued. One pulled a flint knife and jabbed at the other man. Other men held them back, and they quieted. The man left without the cotton.

Muluc had never seen so many different kinds of people: men and women with tattoos and different markings on their faces; women with painted yel-low skin; men with red skin; men wearing great capes; men with shaved heads; men with long hair; women wearing clothing with unfamiliar patterns in every color. Many wore coarse cloth, but others dressed in colorful stitching as elaborate as a king's tomb! And one woman's dress had been embroi-dered to look like jaguar spots. The simple shapes woven in Cobá seemed plain by comparison. Was this the center of the world, where the gods cre-ated the different tribes of men?

As Snake unloaded the baskets and jars that had survived the storm, a man with blue streaks on his face came over. "How many captives did you lose?"

"Five or six," Snake said. "Fierce thunder."

"The gods also took three entire canoes filled with captives." Watching Snake grab Muluc's wrists, the man shook his head. "Separate her—she's elite. Look at her long forehead and lip plug."

"Ahh, but she's dressed like a commoner." Snake fingered Muluc's plain white dress, which had only a few embroidered flowers around the neck. "And her hands are rough." He lifted her hand to show the snakelike mark.

"That's a new wound." The man narrowed his eyes. "Only because you survived the storm will I let you keep her, but don't try to fool me again."

Gagging on the stench of urine, Muluc entered a small, dark hut. In the dim light she recognized the embroidery pattern of girls from Cobá, but there were many other girls as well, speaking different languages and wearing heavy fabrics Muluc had never seen before. Some girls collapsed and slept on the filthy sand floor; the others looked frightened, tired, and hungry. Muluc edged toward the back of the hut and reopened the cut on her lip until a few drops of blood fell into the damp, stinking sand. Would the gods accept such an offering, or would the foul surroundings offend them? Muluc licked her dry lips as she watched the other girls from Cobá cling together. How much of the city had been destroyed?

When the sun flew high in the sky, the door opened and a man with fierce eyes entered, holding a gourd. The other girls scrambled for their turns. With a mouth that felt like it had been stuffed with cotton, Muluc eyed the gourd greedily as it passed to the back of the hut. As she gulped the lukewarm corn gruel, it seemed like another lifetime when she had drunk chocolate and feasted on roasted meats and fresh fruits. When would the warriors from her village rescue her? She hoped a fierce young warrior would save her, fall in love, receive the king's praise with land and spoils, and marry her. She would raise fierce warrior boys whose images would decorate the murals of Cobá's temples. Muluc fell asleep, feeling foolish for fantasizing about some silly romance when she was in such danger. Men bartered outside the hut.

"I'll give you five girls—strong ones—for the basket of jade," Snake said.

"I'll take six, plus a jar of turtle oil."

"Fair trade," Snake said.

The door opened, and a man with long, braided hair entered, picking through the girls, shoving some aside. Muluc crouched against the back wall as the man chose two older girls with thick arms. He examined another girl's hands. "She knows how to work." He nodded.

He spotted Muluc, pulled her roughly to her feet, and brushed his hand across her forehead. She felt faint as her heart beat like a drum.

"Not her," Snake said. "She's going to Chichén."

The man laughed. "You'll never pass her off as a commoner."

Snake grinned. "She can work for me."

Muluc sat down and stared at her hands—the snake-shaped burn formed a hard crust across her palm, but otherwise her palms felt soft. The other captives looked like the slaves who cooked and washed with her mother and made dyes for her father. Where had they come from? They didn't resemble Cobá's children, and their foreheads had not been pressed. Muluc figured the gods had made them to be workers; she'd never once thought they might be stolen. New girls simply appeared in her compound. Her mother always told her to be kind to the slaves, but to expect them to work hard.

Muluc's head began to hurt with painful thoughts. Why wouldn't someone come rescue her? Wouldn't Parrot Nose come after his brother, if not for her? What if Parrot Nose had been killed? Images of warriors rampaging through her family compound filled her mind, but she stopped herself from completing those thoughts as the door swung open again, filling the hut with light.

Snake shoved Muluc and another girl outside. As her eyes adjusted to the bright sunlight, Muluc noticed that the other girl also had a long forehead and a stone in her lip, proving that the warriors had raided another elite compound. Muluc made hand motions to get the girl's attention, but she stared ahead with wide eyes as Snake led them to a canoe loaded with jars of glittering salt and baskets of jade that gleamed like the green lakes of Cobá. Muluc touched the necklace hanging beneath her dress. What had been traded for the jade around her neck? Cotton? Cocoa beans? Turtle oil? Girls?

After Muluc and the other girl had been packed amid the cargo, Snake went to a small hut on the sand and brought out several male captives, including Parrot Nose's brother. Muluc gasped when she saw the deep, festering cuts on the side of his face and the bruises up and down his arms. The canoe rocked in the shallow surf as Cobá's elite climbed in front. Crouched next to a bundle of damp-smelling feathers, Muluc pressed her face into her bent knees and cried, wanting nothing more than to be home in her mother's compound, fixing chocolate for her father.

As the canoe drifted from shore, Muluc saw that tall trees arched over the middle of the island. One tree blossomed with those long-legged pink birds.

• • •

THE DAY 3 BEN
Maize God, Protector of Growing Corn

When the canoe reached land again, Muluc, the warriors, and the traders walked along a rough-cut trail into the jungle. Muluc feared she would collapse from thirst; all she'd had to drink was a bit of corn gruel that had started to sour. Her feet ached and bled from walking on such a rough path, so unlike the smooth white roads of Cobá. Rocks jabbed her feet through the dry dirt, and the sun seared through the thin covering of leaves. The jungle did not grow so lush in this foreign place— weedy vines struggled to grow among the short trees and stunted bushes. All the dust in the air tickled Muluc's nose with a sneeze. She'd heard people talk of other lands, but they always seemed more like stories than anything real. The center of the world was Cobá, wasn't it? A man stumbled ahead of her; the pot he carried cracked, spraying crystals of salt on the road.

"Stop!" Snake glared at the man who had dropped the container. "You will lose your share of salt." He untied Muluc and the other girl. "Pick it up."

Kneeling, Muluc plucked salt from the dusty ground. The other girl met her eyes, her face red with tears. Muluc tried to smile at her, but the girl absent-mindedly scraped her finger through the dirt. One of the warriors came up behind her.

"Faster," he said, nudging the girl with his foot. "I haven't seen my family since the last new moon."

The girl started sobbing. Muluc blinked away her own tears and concentrated on picking up the salt: one handful, two, and three, filling the basket with salt, salt, salt. Tears choked her throat. Salt.

"See, she's a good worker," Snake said, much to his men's amusement. "And she's strong. Watch her carry the salt."

Muluc's arms grew weak as they walked; she felt dizzy and unsteady on her feet. Ahead of her, the path looked hazy, and she shivered even in the hot sun. Pain pounded her head with every wobbly step. The scent of dust filled her nose, and its dryness blanketed her mouth. No shade. The trees grew too short. The road stretched too wide. The other girl stumbled and fell, but Muluc held the basket of salt upright.

"Weak girls!" Snake snatched the basket from Muluc's hands and dribbled water into her mouth.

The world went black.

Muluc woke in darkness. Howler monkeys screamed in the shadowy trees, like angry spirits haunting the woods, but Muluc concentrated on the sound of her breath, her heartbeat. Was she still alive or had she descended into the Otherworld?

Like an answer to her question, Snake emerged from a crude hut and tossed a few cold tortillas at the girls. Nearby, his men sat around a small fire, drinking from gourds and laughing. Snake ordered one of his men to guard the trade goods while the other men disappeared inside the hut. Muluc pillowed her head against a bolt of fabric, wishing that she had the strength to attempt an escape. Maybe after a bit of rest. The other girl slept with her head on Muluc's shoulder. In her state of half sleep, Muluc could hear the men bragging about their trades, while others played a game of chance. She fell asleep to the rhythm of the stones hitting the dirt.

. . .

THE DAY 4 IX
Night and Sacrifice

Birds called to each other as the sky brightened to blue. For a brief moment Muluc felt as if she were back at Cobá. But when she opened her eyes, she found herself surrounded by baskets and bundles. The girl next to her started crying again.

Muluc whispered, "Be strong."

"I want my mother," the girl sobbed.

"She will find you," Muluc said.

"She died trying to save me." The girl wailed like a howler monkey.

Muluc gulped down her own sob.

The guard came and kicked the girl. "Quiet!"

Snake passed a gourd of thin corn gruel around, first to the men, then the girls. Muluc drank until a man snatched the gourd from her lips; she needed strength to escape. The other girl refused to eat.

Did she want to die, like her mother? Small and frail, she looked as if the spirits had stopped protecting her. Muluc hadn't seen anyone killed at Cobá while she was being carried away by her captors, but she had heard the screams. Was that crying infant her brother? The shrieking woman her mother? Muluc shook the memory away, like a dog shakes off water.

All day, in spite of stifling heat, Muluc and the traders trudged through villages and thirsty fields. When the sun began to tilt in the sky so that it shined into their eyes, Muluc saw large stone buildings through the spaces where the jungle had been cleared for planting. The temples burned the color of blood in the descending sun.

Muluc stopped, alert, as if she were standing in front of a mother jaguar. One of Snake's men shoved her, so she stumbled forward, but her heart beat faster with each step she took toward the red city. Surely someone in the city would help her return to Cobá!

Panic tightened Muluc's chest like vines strangling a garden—she dropped her bundle and ran, feet pounding the road so hard that her whole body vibrated. Her breath came in gasps. But she ran and ran. She heard shouts and laughter behind her, but she didn't dare turn around to look. The city still seemed so far away. After several more steps, a sharp pain pinched her waist. She paused, gulping air. A bit of vomit burned in her throat. Then the gruel came pouring out of her mouth, sloshing around her feet.

Snake clasped her wrist, like an eagle snatching a fish from the lake, digging his nails into her flesh. His men laughed and jeered.

"I should smash your skull," Snake hissed, crushing her wrist in his rough hand until she whimpered with pain. "Foolish girl. No one there is going to help you."

Muluc simply stared into his dark, cold eyes.

As they neared the city, the pat-pat-pat of tortilla making filled the air and the smells from cooking fires wafted across the road. Muluc's stomach tightened, pain pinched her temples, and thirst scratched her throat. One foot, then the other—she did not want to faint again.

Just as the sun dropped below the trees in the distance and the Great Star began to shine in the sky, the caravan reached the vast plaza of Chichén. Muluc stared at the four-sided temple with steps going up each side. Though shorter than some of the temples at Cobá, it squatted solidly in the center of everything. Massive red and yellow stone snakes slithered down one stairway to rest their heads on the plaza.

Snake, the warrior, kneeled and pierced his lip, letting a few drops of blood drip onto the stones.

"I have returned," he prayed. "My Lords, I have brought many offerings for your gods and many goods for your people."

People crowded the central plaza—rushing about, chattering like birds. Nearby, Muluc saw a large wall with a small temple connected to a steep stairway. Painted murals covered the wall, and Muluc realized that it formed a ball court. She gasped. Such a gigantic ball court! Cobá had several ball courts, but all of them would have fit inside this one. Muluc felt as small as a mouse in a cornfield. Cobá had grand temples and beautiful murals—most more elaborate—but the size of the plaza gave these temples a look of power and dominance. Did the gods favor Chichén over Cobá?

In the distance, Muluc heard the familiar sound of men dragging large stone blocks up the sides of a new temple. The echoing thuds of temple building used to sound routine to her, almost comforting; she felt pride in the beauty of the temples, comfort in knowing the gods would be pleased with her people. Now the sound echoed deep inside her body in heavy thuds of fear. She stopped walking and took a long breath; the man behind her stepped on her heel, muttering a curse.

"On to the market," Snake said.

Even late in the day, people crowded the market. Women in plain dresses bought small quantities of food, paying with cocoa beans or short lengths of cloth. So many items to trade! A woman wearing shimmering green feathers on her dress argued about the price of vanilla. Muluc inhaled the sweet, rich scent and tried not to think about her mother. The elegant woman briefly glanced down at Muluc: her dusty, tattered dress; crusty vomit clinging to her skin; hair matted like a ragged child's; her bitter scent souring the air. Muluc flushed with shame as the woman averted her eyes. How many times had *she* treated a dirty-looking common girl the same way? Too many.

Some of the men in the group stopped to trade with people in the market, but Snake kept walking. Muluc marveled at the piles of tomatoes, beans, corn, squash, melons, coconuts, and fruits she'd never seen before. The jungle had been so dry, yet these people still had food. Not like the drought in Cobá, when the markets were filled with coconuts, fish, small withered ears of corn, and little else. Muluc did not see much fish here in Chichén—only dry salted fish and turtle. Instead, monkeys, kinkajous, peccaries, rabbits, opossums, deer, turkeys, and pheasants lay piled on reed mats for trade. One woman sat behind a large black-and-white tapir. The aroma of roasting meat from another vendor filled Muluc's dry mouth with saliva while her stomach twisted into a knot of hunger.

At the end of the market, men with long obsidian spears guarded a large building.

"I have captives from the kingdom of Cobá and trade items for the Lords," Snake said.

The inside of the building looked like the gods' market: crammed with more exotic goods than Muluc ever imagined.

A man with long hair braided with a strand of colorful cloth greeted Snake. "You did well," he said, directing the men with salt to a far corner of the building while examining a large pouch of turquoise and jade stones from Snake.

"The Lords will be pleased." The merchant walked among the traders, examining the contents of their baskets, bags, and jars. Each man kept a small portion or traded for something else he wanted. As they finished their business, the traders began to leave. Muluc saw the elite captives—including Parrot Nose's brother—at the far side of the building. They stood with their hands bound, looking strong and fierce in spite of the black and white paint marking them as prisoners. Muluc stood on tiptoe so that they could see her. The merchant prodded them as if they were pigs at the market! Muluc stamped her foot on the stone floor. Parrot Nose's brother looked up. His eyes grew wide as they met hers, but he remained silent and still. Then he lowered his eyes as though ashamed. Why didn't he do something? Attack! Rescue her!

The merchant with the braid whistled and motioned with his hand toward the captives, so the
guards took them away. Parrot Nose's brother
paused, glancing back at Muluc, but a guard jabbed
him with a spear. Muluc watched the blood trickle
down his back, like tears.

The man returned to Snake. "All royals," he
said. "We may have rain yet." He looked at Muluc
and the other girl. "Slaves?"

"Strong girls. They walked all the way from the
island," Snake said.

"We've had a lot of female slaves come in from
the raids," he said. "We need more strong men."
The man lifted the other girl's chin. "This one looks
ill—not fit for work or the gods."

"Just tired," Snake said. "And hungry."

"I'll give you a bag of cocoa beans, some obsidian, feathers—"

"I also want some of the jade for my trouble."

"What about her?" The merchant gestured to
Muluc. "So pretty. She almost looks—"

"I'm taking her for my household," Snake said.
"You said you didn't need more female slaves."

"You'll never get away with having such a pretty
house slave." The man laughed. "Not with your
fierce woman."

Snake's boy gathered the goods while Snake
took the beans and a small piece of jade, clasped

Muluc by the shoulder, and walked away. Muluc squirmed under the firm pressure of his hand.

The sky had darkened when Snake and Muluc walked back through the market. The sellers packed up their goods, taking the exotic fragrances with them. Some carried bundles across the plaza toward the road Muluc had traveled, but this time Snake and Muluc walked in the opposite direction, winding through groups of small temples. The woody smell of copal incense lingered in the air, so that at night the city smelled like Cobá. Muluc closed her eyes for a moment and thought of home, even though it made her throat tighten. Small fires burned in family compounds as she and Snake walked farther from the plaza. She imagined her mother playing with the baby by the hearth fire. Could wishing it make it true?

Snake walked through a short rock wall into a garden where children swarmed him, grabbing his legs, swinging from his arms, hugging his neck.

"My children." He stopped to embrace them and handed them each a piece of dried fruit. "You are growing straight and tall like the Lords' corn."

He continued to walk toward a stone house with a thatched roof. As they entered, Muluc's feet felt dirty on the cool stone floors and her hair felt greasy and tangled as she smoothed it with her hand. Across the room a plump woman reclined on a reed mat, sipping from a clay bowl. Oil burning in little clay pots provided some light, although copal smoke choked the room. A colorful weaving of a battle scene hung on the wall behind the woman—Snake standing over a captive, surrounded by his warriors.

Snake walked to the woman and kneeled before her.

"I have returned, dear one," he said.

He reached into his satchel and brought out the piece of jade. "From the yellow men who travel across the sea." He put the jade up against her skin. "We can carve it with your favorite god, or it would make a good sacrifice."

The woman snatched the jade with her soft, plump hand. "I'll have it for myself," she said. She looked behind Snake. "What is *that?*"

"A slave to make you more comfortable," he said. "She can rub your feet with cocoa butter and help you paint your face."

The woman smiled. "Bring her to me."

Muluc walked to the woman and kneeled as Snake had done. The woman wrinkled her nose. "Do all girls from Cobá stink so? Must be a miserable place." She snorted a laugh, but her smile faded as she touched Muluc's forehead, ran her finger down the jade stone in her nose, and tapped her fat finger on Muluc's lip plug.

"Her forehead is longer than mine—and look at these jewels," she said. "She's obviously elite born and more beautiful than I, even if she is unclean." The woman pouted. "I'll not keep her."

"Her beauty magnifies yours."

The woman narrowed her eyes. Lowering her gaze, Muluc stared at her refection in the polished stone floor. How could the woman think she was beautiful? Filthy. Exhausted. A jagged scab crossed her cheek. Even Parrot Nose might not want her any longer.

"You agree she is beautiful?"

"You said so first," Snake said.

"Harrumph." The woman stood, hefting her round body, fattened with much meat, corn, cocoa, and no work. "I married you when you were just a reckless boy—not the Lords' Great Wandering Warrior."

She plopped back down on her mat. "How many times do I have to remind you that I married beneath myself?" She brought her hand to her forehead.

"Your father is a merchant," Snake said. "I have risen you to the warrior class."

"But you make me suffer," she said. "I'll not keep the girl. Sell her. Buy me jewels like she wears."

"I'm keeping the girl," Snake said. "An elite girl could be worth a lot if handled well."

The woman drew her lips back into a sneer, exposing her teeth, like an angry tusked peccary. "Sell her," she growled.

"Don't you see?" Snake said. "With her we have a connection to the kings of Cobá. If nothing else, she could be valuable for sacrifice."

"Then sell her now and collect your precious jade." Snake's wife rested her head on her arms.

Muluc remained kneeling, as if to fade into the hard, cold stone floor, until Snake yanked her up by the arm. She trembled in his grasp, legs wobbling like a toddler learning to walk.

"We'll talk again in the morning," Snake said to his wife. "I'll take her to sleep in the cook's hut."

The cook splashed a jar of water over Muluc before she would allow her into the cooking hut. Then the cook picked through Muluc's scalp, looking for lice, nearly chopping off her hair. The humiliation! Muluc had always wondered why her mother's new slaves had short hair.

Now she knew.

After putting on a scratchy dress and eating a stale tortilla, Muluc fell asleep on the cool dirt floor like a mangy old dog. At least the dirt absorbed her tears.

CHAPTER SEVEN

"You can't stop the story now, Nando," Barb said as the bus slowed in the parking lot. "What happens to Muluc?"

"I'll tell you more when we get back on the bus," Nando said. "Maybe."

"I just need an eensy-weensy hint." Barb pouted.

"I think you'll live." My thighs made a sucking sound as I lifted them from the seat, and I flapped the front of my shirt to keep it from sticking to me.

"Uh, gross." Talia wrinkled her nose. "Did you forget the antiperspirant?" She waved her hand in front of her nose just like Fiona always did when Grace Williams walked past. Turning toward the cheerleaders, Talia made another joke about me and Nando. More stupid *amor* stuff. Yeah, right. The guy *hated* me. I looked away so she couldn't see my cheeks turn red. Maybe I should just stay on the bus. I couldn't take a whole day of Talia. Or Barb. Or Nando. Or anyone, really.

Alfredo gathered us for an introduction. "Chichén Itzá was big city—a hundred thousand people lived here. Only a few buildings are restored. We explore those today." He looked at Barb. "Stay with the group so we don't lose you."

"I will for sure," Barb said, saluting. And she's the one making friends!

"Just stick with me," Talia said, acting like she'd officially adopted Barb.

"We will go with the guide and see the main buildings, then free time and lunch on the way back. See Mayan dancing," Alfredo said.

I just wanted to go swimming. Take a shower. Take the next plane home.

My shirt, drenched with sweat, stuck to me in a disgusting and embarrassing way. Everyone avoided standing near me. I watched the Bronze Sun Goddess holding hands with Dante; her cheeks flushed pink in the heat, but on her it looked good. I sympathized with some old ladies standing near me under a big tourist bus umbrella. They were wearing stretch pants and long-sleeved blouses. I pulled my shirt from my back and tugged on the bottom of my shorts. My hair, also wet with sweat, clung to my neck. A few gangly trees lined the path, but even the shade felt hot. I gulped some water to avoid heat stroke. Muluc's fainting had sounded a bit dramatic in Nando's story, but now I totally got it. The place was an oven.

We started out at the ball court, and I understood why Muluc felt intimidated. A pair of thick stone walls loomed more than twenty feet above us, stretching down a grassy area wider than a soccer field, capped with crumbling temples on either end. The gray stones, some with mysterious carvings, made me feel tinier than the time our class toured the Utah Jazz basketball arena. Everyone looked small—even Dante and Luc! I couldn't see anything beyond the ancient walls, patchy with moss, and the trees crowding the temples at the end. I snapped several photos of the ball court, but those ladies with their umbrellas kept getting in the way. Besides, I couldn't get the whole thing in one shot, not from the ground anyway. I'd have to sketch it.

"The ball game was sacred to the ancient Mayans," the guide said. "Like basketball to a Lakers fan." He was an older man, short like Nando, but stocky. And funny. I could never be so funny in a second language, let alone a third. I totally messed up the knock-knock jokes we had to present during our Spanish class fiesta. *Muy* embarrassing!

"They played with a ball of rubber made from the sap of the zapote tree, the same tree sap used for chewing gum by Wrigley's last century. Your grandparents chewed it." He looked at the cheerleaders. "Have you ever heard of Chiclets?"

"Sure, we have them in Texas," C.C. said.

"*Chicle* is the Mayan word for chewing."

"Cool." Talia fanned her hair against her neck. Barb imitated her.

"The ball weighed ten pounds." He pointed to a small circle with a hole in it, up at the top of the wall. "To score, they had to get it through there."

I couldn't imagine anyone getting anything through those little stone loops in the wall. Max and Josh faked jump shots.

"You want to take me on?" the guide asked. "But you can't use your hands—just your hips and your feet."

"Sure," they said.

"Even if the loser gets sacrificed?"

Max and Josh flushed red. Everyone laughed. Even me.

The guide walked us over to a panel of stone carvings and showed us a scene of ball game sacrifice. The carvings were so filled with details that it took a while for me to see the players, who wore elaborate feather headdresses, kneepads, and ornaments. Sure enough, in one, a man held a decapitated head. Our guide showed us how the neck of the loser spurted blood in the form of six snakes. He explained that Wak-Kan — or Six Snake — was the name of the Mayans' great World Tree and that all sacrifice had important religious reasons behind it.

"It's not just that they were bloodthirsty, violent people," the guide explained. "The sacrifice of the ball game echoed their myths. It would make your American basketball more interesting, eh? Sacrifice the loser?"

"Sometimes I'd like to sacrifice the referee," Josh said.

I raised my hand, like some dork sitting in a classroom. The guide nodded to me. Talia scoffed, rolling her eyes at Barb, and I almost didn't ask my question, but the guide kept nodding at me, so I did. "Who played the ball games — did they have teams?" I asked.

"Like, duh. Look at the size of this place," Talia said. "As if they'd make one shorty run around this place." She flipped her hair. "It's, like, a *stadium*."

I blushed, hotter, redder.

Barb leaned over to me and said, "You look like a sunburned lobster."

"Shut up, you little brat!" I tried to pinch Barb, but she skittered away, squealing. Nando had a look of disgust on his face that made him look *worse* than one of those creepy carvings. Why does he care anyway? To him we're just dumb tourists.

The guide cleared his throat. "Yes, the Mayans played with two teams: the warriors and the captives. Ball games were political and religious," he said. "Many times kings would capture other rulers from different cities, and they would settle their differences on the ball court. Or a king could make himself more powerful by sacrificing another ruler's elite to the gods after a ball game."

I felt a little shiver of worry for Parrot Nose's brother. But then I felt totally stupid. Why did I care about some silly story Nando made up? I only listened to it because there was absolutely nothing else to do on that stupid, boring bus.

"Guess they didn't need cheerleaders," Talia said to C.C. and Jessie, but they ignored her.

"The elite watched the ball games from these two temples, but others could sit on top of the wall and watch." The guide moved forward. "Let's continue."

"Your shirt is *so* sweaty," Talia said to me as we walked through the crowds of people to another section of the ruins.

"Yeah," Barb echoed.

I growled low, "You're like a little parrot—imitating her all the time. It makes you a total brat when you laugh at her mean jokes. Like yesterday—"

"But it's true!" Barb said. "You look like Dad after he's played basketball."

I shoved Barb hard enough to make her stumble. "Shut up!"

Nando looked at me, all wide-eyed and shocked. "Are you okay?" he asked Barb, completely ignoring the fact that I was actually sticking up for him!

I marched ahead, letting them stare at my disgusting sweaty shirt.

The guide led us along the path near the big pyramid. The steps looked so steep, and I pictured myself slipping, tumbling backwards, and breaking 203 of my 206 bones. Thankfully, the whole thing was roped off, so even Barb couldn't get any ideas. I tried taking another picture, but there were just so many people crowding around. I mentally added a new reason to my journal, number 48: too many tourists!

"There are too many people," I said. "I want to see it like it was."

"With a hundred thousand people, I think it would have been even more crowded back then." Nando looked at me like my intelligence hovered around 2.3. "There are maybe a thousand people here right now." Nando glanced around as if he were counting.

"I just mean— It would be cool to see real Mayans," I said, probably lowering my intelligence score to a 1.7.

Nando stood in front of me, faking a big, cheesy grin. "That's what you want? Okay, take your snapshot of the happy little native boy."

"That's not what I meant." My face felt like it might burst into flame, so I gulped the rest of the water I'd brought. Chances of contracting heat stroke now: eighty percent.

"We should start sacrificing rich American *turistas*," Nando muttered. "*If* the gods would have them."

. . .

We walked through the searing heat until we stood in front of a pyramid with a round dome on top. Barb ran ahead of the group, begging me to take her picture. I refused, but then Talia handed her camera to Nando and got him to snap a picture of her and Barb. Let them have their chummy little photo — there was nothing about this day that I wanted to remember.

"This is the observatory," our guide said, "or El Caracol, because the Spanish thought it looked like a snail, with its round walls and spiral staircase. The Mayans were great astronomers; they knew the sky so well that their calendar was actually more exact than the one we use today. They were also great mathematicians. Did you know the Mayans invented the concept of zero?"

The ancient Mayans would have loved me: a big, fat zero.

With Barb still at her side, Talia slung her arm through Luc's and whispered in his ear. Why wasn't she listening? Even the ancient Mayans were intelligent. She kept making fun of Nando and Alfredo because they had accents, yet somehow Luc's didn't seem to bother her.

We walked back toward the center of the plaza, past the pyramid again. I wondered why they'd closed it to tourists. Too many deaths? We kept trudging along in the heat (I'd lost like seventy-five percent of my body water) until we were on a long white chalky tree-lined road that led to a massive green well of slimy-looking water. It was as round as a giant's bowl of pea soup and as wide across as our hotel's largest pool (not that *anyone* would want to swim in water the color of infected pus). Trees, bushes, and vines nervously peered over the edge across from us; we stood near a small stone platform that looked way too much like a diving board.

"You are now at the sacred cenote." Our guide swung his hands wide. "Mayans today still occasionally make sacrifices to this well. A cenote is a collapsed cave above an underground river. The Yucatán Peninsula is covered with limestone. There are no surface rivers, but there is an extensive network of underground rivers and caves and many cenotes. So watch out if you're wandering around in the jungle." He laughed. "You might fall in. Sacrifice yourself by accident."

"It smells like something's rotting around here," I said.

Nando made a snuffing sound through his nose. That was disgusting too.

Talia simply said, "You're probably just smelling yourself."

Barb laughed—even after what I'd said to her!

We walked closer and gaped at the thick, almost greasy-looking green water about twenty feet down. The rocky sides were the color of gravestones—whitish with smudgy black areas. Scrubby bushes grew from the cracks in the pocked stone.

"The Mayans *did* sacrifice people here, but not just virgins, like some guides like to tell tourists. Not me, I'm honest." He put his hand on his chest and crossed his heart. "The Mayans sacrificed everybody." He stopped and pointed at each one of us. "Yes, all of you would make good sacrifices. Any volunteers?"

The guys laughed. Josh grabbed C.C.'s arm and pretended

to sacrifice her. "No way are you *even* going to try to get me into that foul hole," she said.

"Just think of all the rotting bodies," Josh teased.

Everyone started adding their own descriptions: decapitated skulls, flesh dripping with slime, hands reaching out to grab you. The guide took it all in stride, but Nando's face darkened to an angry red.

"It *is* pretty gross," I said, but Nando shot a poisoned look at me.

He muttered, "It is *sacred*."

The guide ignored all the sacrificial pushing and shoving, and continued. "Many many years ago, a man decided to dredge the cenote. They found bones from people of all ages, plus gold and many other treasures."

"Did they find all the gold?" Barb asked.

Not again!

"No, the cenote is very deep—about one hundred feet—and the bottom is covered with hundreds of years of trees and debris, plus the current of the river makes it dangerous. We'll probably never find everything."

Barb walked out to the very edge, but I yanked the back of her shirt.

"Don't even think about it," I said. "There is no way I'm rescuing you in that green swamp of ancient rotting bodies, even if there is gold a hundred feet down."

"Yeah. Besides, you'd *never* be able to get back out," Talia said. "And you couldn't get Dante to come to your rescue this time either."

"I just know there's treasure down there," Barb said. "I just know it."

"So go to graduate school, or make a million dollars and come back with all your fancy equipment." I pulled her next to me. *"Not now."*

Talia smirked at me. "Quit stressing. It's not like she's serious."

But then Barb asked, "Does anyone ever swim here?"

I rolled my eyes at Talia, but she was too busy watching Josh flirt with C.C.

"No, this cenote is sacred," the guide said. "The Mayans didn't even get their water here. They used another one closer to the plaza. Look, the walls are steep; just the fall alone killed most of the sacrificial victims."

Barb looked unconvinced. "It's so hot, a swim would feel great."

"Nice try," I said.

"Come on, Barbie," Talia said. "I'll take you swimming when we get to the hotel."

"Promise?" Barb asked.

Barbie? She *hates* that nickname!

"I can take my own sister swimming," I said, but Talia looked at me like she wasn't so sure.

"But you'll be too busy writing postcards to your zillions of friends back home," she said. "Barbie tells me everything." She nodded her head toward Barb, still gawking at the cenote. "Plus, it's not like you're exactly athletic. *I'm* teaching her the backstroke."

I sauntered up next to Barb to hide my blushing cheeks—and pinched her arm hard.

"Since you're such a blabbermouth, Barb, why *don't* you go for a swim?" I lowered my voice. "And stop talking about me, or I'll sacrifice you myself."

"Ouch! I'm telling Mom." Barb ran to catch up with Talia.

Nando gave me another dirty look. Why does he care? It's none of his business anyway.

I brushed past him, trying my best to catch up with the group without breaking into a run. I felt like such a little kid—just like the time Fiona made us all speed walk around the mall like the old people. I couldn't keep up. I never kept up. Fiona called me "oh-so retirement home ready." Talia's right, I'm not athletic. I can't do anything! I'm even dumb when it comes to all the Mayan culture stuff, asking stupid questions, making Nando mad.

The guide stopped at the bottom of El Castillo, the big pyramid, and blabbered on about how the pyramid has ninety-one steps on each side, plus one more at the top. "It all adds up to three hunded and sixty-five, same as the days of the year. See? Weren't those ancient Mayans smart? Okay, time for some photos and—"

"Good thing we can't climb. Kat's legs aren't long enough," Talia said.

"She'd be too chicken anyway," Barb said.

That's it!

I slipped under the rope blocking off the pyramid. "Hey!" the guide shouted, but his voice grew faint in my ears as I leaped up the steep steps, still glossy polished marble in places. My thighs started to burn, but I didn't even look down, I just kept going. Why was Talia trying to turn my own sister against me? Why did everyone treat me like such a baby? And why did I feel like such an idiot around Nando—he's no Zach B.! Next year I hoped Zach B. would finally notice *me* and not just joke around with Fiona all the time. What if Fiona and her precious Five crank call him from mini-camp? Or what if they meet up at the movies with his friends? I pictured Fiona going out with Zach B., holding hands in the hall, slow dancing at the holiday formal, doing homework together at the library, even though Fiona called libraries "oh-so Dullsville." *I can't take it anymore!*

I pounded my anger into each step. My breath came fast, and my chest hurt, but I didn't care. *I'd rather die from some freak heart attack up here than suffer another minute with Talia and her precious Barbie.* Sliding a bit, I grabbed the step in front of me and pulled myself to the top. Sweat dripped from my forehead into my eyes. Hands on my knees, I sucked in gulps of air, then flapped my shirt to create a breeze. How hot could someone get before bursting into flames? Turning around, I felt dizzy as I stared out across miles of green—the whole world rolled out to the horizon in one long green shag carpet. I towered over the other pyramids.

From up here, the steps looked even steeper. How would I get down? Clinging to the wall, I slipped into the little room built on top of the pyramid. Thick black soot darkened the walls, and I crinkled my nose at the smell of the hot, dank air. I traced my name across the blackened walls, wondering if all this soot was left over from ancient prayers and offerings. I closed my eyes and whispered my own short prayer: "Please let eighth grade be different."

I walked back out, squinting in the hot sunshine. How did those short ancient people get down from these steps? Or was this pyramid another form of sacrifice? I waved at Nando and the others, who stood staring at me from the bottom. Nando shook his fist at me. The guide shouted something that didn't sound friendly.

But I ignored them and walked around to the other side of the pyramid, overlooking the Temple of the Warriors with its forest of carved columns, and tried to imagine it as a thriving marketplace. Muluc saw all this when it was new and painted with bright colors. Today it seemed like such a gray place. If only I could zip back in time and see it all painted red, blue, and yellow. Plus, I could help Muluc. Were they going to dump her into that nasty green water? Nando *would* tell a story like that.

I breathed in the hot air at the highest point in Chichén Itzá, thinking that I wasn't going to allow people to make me feel beneath them anymore. Starting now with Talia. And Nando. And even stupid, traitorous Barb. My heart thudded as I looked down the steep steps, wondering if someone could maybe send a helicopter to get me off of this thing. How many tourists break their necks climbing pyramids? I'm sure that's why they closed it. I imagined thunking down the steps the way I'd skidded on the stairs at the movies, popcorn flying everywhere and Fiona laughing her head off because I was "oh-so stairway-challenged." But I thought of Muluc struggling to stay strong, and I took a deep breath, counted to ten, and counted to ten again. Then I just did it.

I walked down like they were any old stairs.

Our whole tour group cheered for me—except Nando.

"You've got the guts," Dante said with his sexy accent, staring down at my legs. "Strong."

"Thanks." Does blushing increase your chances of spontaneous combustion? Dante offered me his water bottle. I took a long drink, and his fingers brushed mine when I handed it back, causing my whole body to tingle, alive and triumphant. Is this what it feels like to win an Olympic medal or something?

"Dang, how did you *do* that?" Josh asked. "How did those tiny Mayan people do this all the time, wearing all those feathers and capes?"

"Maybe that's the trick," I said. "You have to be small."

"Small, but strong as hell," Josh said. "You're amazing."

Nando spat out, "She's a disrespectful tourist. The worst kind. Using our temples like a playground. Not caring about our culture—just wants to come take her pretty pictures."

Did he have tears in his eyes?

"Gosh, I'm sorry." My stomach fluttered almost as bad as it did on top of the pyramid. "I didn't hurt it. I didn't even take any pictures, but how could that hurt anything anyway?"

"That's not the point. You didn't care. You rich Americans don't care." Nando turned on his heel and stomped away, still cursing me.

The guide pushed through the group and continued to scold me, blending Spanish-English-Mayan, and that's when Alfredo decided the tour had better be over. No one really complained, because we'd seen the highlights and it was like a million degrees outside. The Bronze Sun Goddess actually thanked me as we walked back to the bus in the sweltering afternoon sun.

But Nando wouldn't even look at me.

Barb kept begging him to continue the story, but he wouldn't look at her either. And even though she's a total pain, it made me mad. Barb didn't do anything to him or his precious been-there-for-hundreds-of-years-withstood-thousands-and-thousands-of-tourists pyramid.

"Hey, tell her the story," I said when we sat down in the bus. Even though Josh invited me to sit back with the group, I sat next to Barb because she was upset, not that I cared *that* much, but *I* was her sister and I wasn't about to let Talia take over. Not anymore.

"You don't care about my story," Nando said. "You're just bored. You don't have your American television out here in the jungle. I'm just a clown to you."

"Omigosh, Nando. I apologized. I'm really sorry that I climbed the pyramid." My shoulders sagged. "Even though I totally didn't hurt anything."

"Yeah? Well plenty of tourists have—someone damaged the Chac Mool, jumping on it like playground equipment."

"But I didn't."

"But you have the same attitude."

"No, I don't—"

Nando turned around, and I could see the hurt in his eyes. He was right. I didn't respect the boundaries. I just did what I wanted—kind of like Fiona.

I peeped, "I am sorry, okay?"

I felt a million times smaller than I did standing in the great ball court.

Barb touched Nando's shoulder. "Please tell me the story. I have so much respect for your cultural heritage, and I'm here to learn and expand my mind." She totally copied something that Mom had said, but Nando simply raised his eyebrows and sighed.

"I'm telling this for you. Not her." Nando glanced at me. Barb took that as an invitation to jump up to Nando's seat. I stayed behind, watching the jungle through the windows. From the top of the pyramid it had looked almost smooth, but down here everything was far more complicated—tangles and tangles of life.

"So, Muluc was staying at that Snake guy's house," Barb said. "He's like meaner than the bad guy from—"

"My story is much better than your American television."

I leaned forward so I could hear as Nando started telling the story. Riding on the bus *was* totally boring.

• • •

THE DAY 5 MEN
Elderly Moon Goddess, Waning Phase of the Moon
Muluc woke to the sound of Snake arguing with his peccary woman. When the crash of a clay pot shattering echoed throughout the compound, Muluc crept to the main room, peeked around the corner, and watched Snake's wife lift an incense

burner above her head. It was shaped like a sturdy warrior.

"Do not dishonor our family gods." Snake's voice trembled.

The incense burner struck the stone floor, the warrior's body breaking into pieces. One of his large round ear ornaments skipped across the floor near Muluc.

"I can replace that old pot," the woman yelled. "You will not dishonor *me* by bringing home pretty young slaves." She brushed her hand across the altar, tipping a carved vase to the floor. The feather-adorned Lord on the vase split in two.

"That was a gift from the Lords' Council," Snake hissed, picking up a pottery shard from the floor and flinging it at his wife. She squealed as a few drops of blood bubbled up on her arm.

"You will not threaten me!" She threw the next vase at Snake, but he caught the slender vessel before it struck him.

"The girl stays." Snake glared at his wife, then turned and strode out of the compound.

Muluc sneaked back to the cooking hut, cringing at the thought of living in a house where the gods suffered dishonor. The gods would bring sickness, or worse. She stayed in the kitchen, crouched on the floor like a dog.

The cook came and began making *atole*—a

warm cornmeal drink—then fresh tortillas with honey. And chocolate. Muluc's mouth watered as the spicy smell of hot chocolate warmed the air. Girls came in and fetched platters of food.

Muluc had spent no time in her own family's cooking hut. The food appeared; she ate what she wished. Even in drought, when the food became monotonous, she had never suffered hunger, not like she had these past few days. The cook tossed a misshapen tortilla to Muluc.

"The lady will not keep you," the cook said. "She's very jealous and worries about her fading beauty." She motioned for Muluc to stand and handed her a gourd of water, not chocolate, and another overcooked tortilla. "But you might as well work while you're here," she said.

All morning Muluc helped the cook and her girls slice tomatoes, peppers, and potatoes; shell beans; stew meat. The cook kept scolding her for making mistakes and not knowing how to prepare even the simple dishes. Snake and his family ate well, especially for such a dry rainy season.

Later in the day, Muluc heard the piggish woman's heavy footsteps approaching.

"She's with the cook, eating, getting strong," Snake's wife said.

Muluc quickly kneeled, spit in the dirt, rubbed a little mud onto her finger, and smeared it across her lip plug and the jewels in her nose and ears.

"She has the strange looks of Cobá. They even press common babies' skulls, but she is strong." Snake's wife entered the hut with another woman. "She will be a good worker."

Muluc stood straight but cast her eyes to the ground.

"You're very generous, but I don't think I can—" The woman spoke in a quiet voice.

"Take her," Snake's wife said. "You can have her for almost nothing."

The woman's forehead crinkled. "How much?"

"How about three vases and a clay incense burner? My son accidentally broke some things on the family altar, tossing a ball in the house," she said. "I do not want his father to be angry with him—nor the gods."

"I don't know." The woman took Muluc's hands in her own. "She does have delicate hands, maybe good for forming pots."

"Yes, her hands are lovely." Snake's wife blew her breath out through her nose. "Take her. I insist."

"I will send the items with my boy before sundown." The woman bowed, glancing at Muluc with a confused expression on her face. "Thank you, kind mistress."

Snake's wife narrowed her beady eyes. "It's my pleasure."

Muluc and her new owner, a tiny, wiry woman with calloused hands, walked through the Great

Plaza near the traders' road, but they continued deep into the jungle. The huts grew farther apart and poorer, all wood and thatch with dirt floors.

"I don't know why she sent for me," the woman said. "I've never sold to a warrior before—and at such a price." She looked at Muluc. "I can use the help, I guess, with the big ceremony and all the pots needed." She shook her head. "You never know the way of the gods."

Muluc thought the woman's voice sounded kind even though she had tired eyes and wore a thread-bare dress. Once she had gained some strength, Muluc felt certain she could escape.

They approached a small wooden hut with a wide yard enclosed by a short rock wall. The place did not look busy like the other family compounds they had passed, but the air felt hot and stagnant with the stink of burning clay. A dog lay in the dirt, sleeping through their arrival. A few rangy ramon and avocado trees grew above a dry-looking garden: small hard squashes, scant tomatoes, some beans and corn, a few chilies. Muluc did not expect to relieve her hunger here.

The woman walked into the hut, leaving Muluc standing in the yard. The dog lifted his head, flopped his chin back onto the dirt, closed his eyes, and slept. The woman returned with three small vases and an incense bowl. None as beautiful as those

Snake's wife had broken. She whistled, and a small dust-covered boy appeared.

"Take these to the warrior's house—the one with the snake winding around his neck." The boy's eyes grew wide. "Yes, the warrior from the parade." She handed him the bowls. "Be careful."

"Who's she?"

"That warrior's crazy lady gave me this girl for the bowls," she said. "I don't know why, when I would've preferred cornmeal to another mouth to feed."

Muluc knew why.

• • •

THE DAY 6 CIB
Vulture

Muluc fell asleep remembering the marriage feast of the king's son: chocolate, roast peccary, roasted birds, stewed deer, potatoes, tomatoes, tamales, coconut, chocolate . . . Her wedding feast with Parrot Nose would be the same, except she'd request more chocolate. But then owls swarmed into her dream, their faces painted with blue streaks, like the warriors from Chichén, and her mother screamed as the owls flew off with the baby clutched in their furry talons. One of the owls had a snake for a head and hissed at Muluc.

She sat up, startled in the darkness, her heart beating fast. Listening to the eerie sounds of night creatures creeping near the house, she tried to go back to sleep. A jaguar growled. Muluc froze. Finally, focusing on the easy sounds of breathing coming from the wiry woman, Macaw, and her thin boy, Mol, she slept again, falling asleep just before daylight.

Macaw and Mol had gone when Muluc finally tore herself from sleep late in the morning. Spider monkeys prattled in the trees. The dog barked in the yard, and Muluc guessed the monkeys had swung in to steal avocados. Back and neck aching, she sat up from her thin, worn mat on the dirt floor. A small fire burned in the three hearthstones in the center of the hut, reminding Muluc of last night's tortillas made from starchy ramon instead of corn. She'd gagged on them. No one in Cobá ate so poorly! Did they?

Feeling a bit dizzy, Muluc walked into the yard to look for Macaw, but only the dog lay sleeping in his usual position, as if he were a clay figure. Muluc walked over to the dog and nudged him with her foot; he sneezed, but didn't move, so Muluc went around the back of the hut to look for Macaw.

"Who are you?" A man's voice called to her from the road. "What are you doing?" A short man with thick arms entered the yard.

As he approached, Muluc saw that he was only

a few years older than she, but his body had grown thick and strong from hard labor, and he had short-cropped hair in the style of stonecutters. "Answer me, girl," he said. "Who are you?"

"I'm here to work," she said in a shaky voice. In Cobá she'd never respond to such a rude commoner!

"My mother cannot afford help," he said. "Where *is* my mother?"

"I don't know," Muluc said. "I just woke up."

"Some help." He tilted his head and looked at her, blushing the color of dried chilies before averting his eyes in a way that pleased Muluc's elite vanity. "You are not from Chichén." He glanced up at her shyly. "But you don't really look like a slave."

Slave. Tears blurred Muluc's vision before dropping onto her cheeks, and she felt lightheaded as images from her nightmare swirled in her mind, confusing past with present, dream from reality, life from death. Was she dead? Was he a guardian of the Otherworld, Xibalba?

He took one of Muluc's hands gently, tracing his calloused finger across her smooth palm. "You've never worked a day in your life." He spoke in a whisper. "Where are you from?"

Muluc shook her head. Cobá. She could not utter such a beautiful word in such a dry, forlorn place.

"What is your name, then?"

"Muluc," she said, gathering strength as the sky collects clouds before a storm. "I was stolen, traded, and now I'm here." Remembering her noble birth, she looked him in the face. "I don't know why."

"My name is Balam."

Thinking that his powerful body *did* resemble a jaguar's, Muluc flushed as she looked into his dark brown eyes, kind like his mother's. He kept his eyes locked in Muluc's bold gaze, but did not leer at her with greed as Snake had done.

"My mother is probably gathering clay," he said a moment later. "Have you eaten?"

Muluc shook her head, so Balam plucked avocados from the tree and picked a couple of reddish-green tomatoes from the garden, then walked into the hut.

"Any tortillas left from last night?"

Muluc pointed to a small basket near the grinding stone.

"Ramon?" he asked. "She doesn't have any corn left?"

"I don't know. I just got here."

Balam threw the tortilla back into the basket. "I knew she wouldn't get the corn planted without me."

"Where have you been?"

"Building another temple for the gods," he said. "Warriors came and took me from my mat one morning, not caring that my father had just died."

Biting into a hard tomato, Muluc tried to keep her thoughts away from her own family. The image of her father working in his studio, paint spots splattered on the cool marble floors, popped into her head—her mother in a crisp white gown walking to the market, passing by the colorful murals on the great temples. Cobá. She saw the tall green trees, shimmering lagoons, and bright temples painted with the stories of the gods, warriors, and kings from the beginning of time.

"The Lords worked him to death, carrying all that stone," Balam said. "His body shrunk with dragging those heavy blocks. His neck almost disappeared as he shrunk to the size of a boy. Then a stone fell from its ropes and crushed his leg."

The avocado skins cracked and sizzled as Balam threw them into the fire. He handed Muluc a thick slice, and she devoured it in two bites, even though it was not quite ripe. At home, her mother would've scolded a slave who served unripe fruit.

"His friends carried him back here in the middle of the night so he could die with his family." Balam grimaced as he bit into his bitter slice of avocado. "Some men who die are buried within the temple walls—sacrificed to the gods."

Muluc blinked back tears, thinking about her own father. She couldn't imagine losing him. "I didn't know."

"How could you? You just got here."

"No. I mean, I didn't know."

Surely the temples of Cobá were not built with the blood of boys' fathers.

. . .

THE DAY 4 AHAU
Sun, Lord

Many cycles of the Great Star passed, and Muluc grew used to her work with the potter's family. She helped Balam in the *milpa* by weeding the field while he planted seed corn in the ground using a pointed digging stick. The thin soil barely covered the rocky earth, so they could not plant in neat rows—only where there was enough soil to cover a seed. Around the corn, they planted squash and beans, then prayed for rain.

They watered their plants with their nighttime waste and sometimes hiked deep down into the earth near the sacred river—where Macaw gathered clay—to bring pots of water to the corn. Muluc hated going down to the deep cenote, so close to the Otherworld Xibalba. In the evenings they burned incense at the family altar and offered small portions of their meager meals to the rain gods. The corn would feed no one if the gods did not give rain.

Muluc also helped Macaw make pots, incense

burners, bowls, and sometimes little figures of the rain god Chac. Rain had not fallen for many cycles, and the Lords of Chichén called on the craftsmen to make figures for a ceremony in the plaza on the day 4 Ben.

They worked until the sun left no trace of light in the sky, and because Macaw did not have oil, they sometimes worked in the yard near a small fire so they could have some light. Many nights they fell into exhausted sleep on their mats, but with only ten days until the ceremony, they worked hard to craft a crowd of Chac statues.

One night Muluc formed the long, curling snout of the reptilian Chac figure.

"You do that so naturally," Balam said. "Are you sure you're not the monkey craftsman from Xibalba?"

Muluc enjoyed using her hands to create images of the gods. Now she understood why Parrot Nose always lingered around her father: to make those beautiful books full of stories and color would feel like walking with the gods.

"We could paint them," she said, thinking of all the pots of dye and paint in her father's studio.

"Nothing to trade for dye," Macaw said.

Muluc looked down at her Chac and pinched two little fangs so they curved into his mouth. Using the quill of a feather, she carved his eyes into the soft clay before adding clay to form his body and sturdy little legs. Last, she carved clothes onto his body with the quill and added a small ear of corn to his leg above the glyph for Chen, the date of the Lords' big rain ceremony.

Balam pointed to the glyph. "What is that?"

"The date sign for the ceremony," she said.

"How do you know?" he asked.

"What are you doing?" Macaw asked.

"I added it for luck," Muluc said. "Maybe we could sell some at the market."

Macaw walked over to the other side of the fire, where Muluc and Balam sat. She peered at Muluc's figure.

"How did you learn to read?" she asked.

"I'm only copying something I saw somewhere once," Muluc said quickly. "I thought it looked pretty with its three little moons inside."

"Let's keep them simple, but I like the idea of selling them at the market." She sat back down next to Balam's little brother, Mol. "With your help, Muluc, we will have more than the Lords' share." She nodded toward the small cornfield. "And if no rain comes, we could use some dry corn to eat." She paused. "I know you must not be used to ramon tortillas."

"Your tortillas are good," Muluc said to be polite.

"You lie," Balam said, nudging Muluc with his

elbow. "But we'll have corn soon. The gods will be pleased with our work and the Lords' ceremony."

"You are kind to me, my little raindrop," Macaw said, smiling at Muluc.

Muluc carried the figure to the clay box in the pit where the figures and bowls were fired. She was not used to working hard, but she found satisfaction in making things with her hands and using her body to work for the gods. Alhough she still missed her family, waited for someone to rescue her, and sometimes thought of escaping, she wasn't afraid anymore. And she had not dreamed of owls since that first night. Now she dreamed of making small figures or weeding between tiny emerging corn plants—all repetitive dreams, reliving her repetitive tasks, but happy.

Sometimes she dreamed that she was Macaw's daughter. Once, she even dreamed that she was Balam's wife and the yard sang with the laughter of children.

• • •

THE DAY 5 IMIX
Crocodile
Early the next morning, Muluc slipped out of the hut, quiet as a cat, creeping through the jungle, staying close to the trail leading to the cenote but

veering far enough to find wildflowers. She collected pink impatiens in her skirt, always leaving one or two flowers on the plants for the gods. As she walked, she tried to remember how her father's workers made the blue dye for the bark scrolls. A red-breasted quetzal with long green iridescent tail feathers landed on a branch above her and began to sing.

Listening, Muluc closed her eyes. The image of her father working in his studio flashed into her head, and she knew she would be able to make paint.

"Thank you," Muluc whispered to the bird. She gathered more flowers and berries and raced back to the yard.

Singing as if to imitate the bird's song, Muluc burned the flowers in a small clay bowl until they turned a shade of light turquoise, the color of seawater. In other pots she made red and yellow paint.

With wet clay Muluc began to form a figure with her hands, larger than the others she had made—an incense burner that looked like a ball-game warrior. Thick plugs in his lips, huge sun disks dangling from his ears, a cape flowing behind him, a grand shield hanging across his chest, and a heavy leather skirt: the figure emerged from her hands as if the gods spoke through her.

Muluc painted the figure bright colors. On the shield she wrote the name of the maize god; on the skirt she drew the maize god emerging from the Otherworld during the fourth creation. She painted the sun disks yellow mixed with red, adding turquoise snakes. She painted more blue streaks across the warrior's cheeks.

"How—" Balam asked.

Not shifting her focus, Muluc continued to paint as she had seen her father do when he got that look on his face, as if his thoughts were in the Otherworld.

"A bird spoke to me," she finally said.

Muluc worked all day, creating figures and painting them with elaborate designs to honor the rain gods, the maize gods, and the ballplayers. Painting the symbols from the stories her father and mother told about creation made her feel connected to Cobá. Finally, she painted the stories that all could read in the sky.

• • •

THE DAY 2 CHUEN
Monkey—the Great Craftsman,
Patron of the Arts and Knowledge
A good day.

Before sunrise Muluc and Balam gathered the best of the figures to bring to market. They walked all the way to Chichén, carrying the figures in baskets on their backs or hung from their foreheads by tumplines. Mol had gathered leaves in the jungle to cushion the figures on their journey.

"The baskets are so heavy." Muluc's neck strained under the load, and her shoulders ached the longer they walked. Now she knew why so many old slaves walked with bent backs.

"Nothing compared to stone," Balam said.

"I shouldn't complain," Muluc said, not wanting to insult Balam.

"You will get used to it. Look how strong you have become."

Muluc smiled, although she feared that her body would grow misshapen and ugly before she even married. Her cocoa-colored skin had already darkened with too much sun; her slender arms had grown thick as a stonecutter's; her feet had toughened to a texture resembling tree bark; and her hands . . .

Other families joined them on the road, taking their wares to market. The Lords had proclaimed 2 Chuen as an auspicious market day before the rain ceremony to honor the Chacs, and the Great Plaza flowed with people. As sellers set up their goods on rows of mats, Muluc saw as many different kinds of people as she had seen on the island. Women with feathered gowns clustered around merchants selling turquoise from a land far north, where the red men lived. Other people shopped for exotic food to prepare for the family feasts before the ceremony. Even

Macaw told Muluc to trade for some corn, cocoa beans, and pom incense. And maybe some meat.

"Please get something for yourself," Macaw said. "Something to remind you of your home, maybe."

Muluc knew that she had grown distant from Macaw and Balam; sometimes Mol couldn't even make her smile. Painting had reminded her of her father more than ever, and her mother had become a constant companion, whispering encouragement into her dreams. Even Parrot Nose popped into her thoughts, and she had started thinking of him by his real name, Quetzal. She missed home with a longing as fierce as the jaguar's hunger for meat.

A small crowd gathered as Balam spread their thin reed mat on the stones and began to unpack Muluc's figures and incense burners.

A woman with beautiful embroidery on her dress picked up a warrior incense burner. "Fine work," she said to Balam. "Who is your father?"

"He lives with the gods in the Otherworld," he said.

"He taught you well," she said.

"Actually—"

"Actually, Balam does very fine work indeed," Muluc said. "He is too modest."

The woman gave Balam a small obsidian knife for the incense burner and a few smaller pieces.

"You're going to make us rich," he whispered to Muluc.

By midmorning they had sold most of the bigger pieces. Only a few small, unpainted bowls, glazed with plain red clay, remained scattered on the mat.

"I'll trade the rest of these," Balam said. "Why don't you take some of these cocoa beans and find something for yourself?"

"I don't know," Muluc said. How could she buy something trivial when it would cost so much? "I can't think of anything."

"Go look around." Balam touched her arm. "You can at least buy us something special to eat. I've never had so much to trade."

Walking down the long rows between the merchants selling everything from avocados to rare sea creatures used for medicine, Muluc finally stopped and traded for two tamales stuffed with roasted peccary, for herself and Balam. She carried them back to the mat with coconuts to drink.

"Such a fancy lunch," he said. "Fit for a Lord."

Muluc enjoyed the best meal she had eaten in days, although the tamale was a little bland. At Cobá, she would have complained to the cook and demanded another, but now it simply tasted good.

"Go look around some more," Balam said, licking his fingers. "We only have three small bowls left to trade."

Her appetite awakened, Muluc said, "Maybe something sweet?"

"Wonderful," he said.

Muluc wandered farther from the mat. Passing a seller with baskets of feathers, she chose a single red feather for Macaw; at another place she traded some cocoa beans for two small carved wooden warriors for Mol, which she tied into the hem of her skirt; and at the end of the row she spotted a small painted jaguar perfect for Balam. She blushed as she handed the cocoa beans to the vendor.

Holding the small jaguar in her hand, Muluc headed down the next row, toward the sweet smell of honey and fried tortillas. She walked past several women selling flowers, shells, and feathers used in making dye, and paused in front of some purple sea urchins. Fingering the sharp spines, Muluc imagined the color she could create.

"Ahh, is it really you? The girl with the spirit of thunder?"

The blind market woman from her mother's chamber! A shock of lightning flamed through Muluc's limbs.

"I feel your presence," the blind woman said. "The jaguar guards you."

Muluc looked at the jaguar in her hand. Could the woman see it? Muluc held the small painted jaguar up, but the woman's cloudy eyes did not blink. She spoke again in a low voice. "Remember your spirit is thunder, but the jaguar guards you."

Muluc wanted to turn and run, but her feet stuck to the stones in the plaza. Words spun loose on her tongue. She needed to ask, but she feared the question would emerge as a wail.

A group of royal women stopped to look at the urchins. Pushing Muluc away, a bejeweled woman asked, "How much?"

"What do you have?" The blind woman negotiated.

Head pounding with memories, Muluc stepped away.

The woman reached her gnarled hand toward Muluc. "Not yet."

"I'm talking to you," the royal woman said. "Ignore the common girl."

"Common?" The blind woman shook her head. "She is a queen."

Muluc felt another shiver in her blood.

The royal woman laughed. "She's so common the gods wouldn't even take her for sacrifice." The woman stared at the stone in Muluc's lip for a moment, shaking her head slightly. "Do not be rude to me, you blind fool, or I'll get a guard."

"No need," the blind woman said. "Please take an urchin, my courtesy."

Eagerly snatching her prize, the woman passed the urchin to her slave. "That's more like it," she said with a huff.

"Dark spirit." The blind woman shook her head. "Chills my bones. But you, you—"

Muluc kneeled down at the edge of the mat, pretending to examine an urchin.

"My mother?" she whispered.

"No fear. The warriors protected the royal compounds. Few were captured."

"Tell her—"

"I'll not return." The woman rubbed her eyes. "I feel it." Again the clouded eyes stared at Muluc. "But you will."

"I can't—I don't know how. Please tell my mother—"

"Listen, and you will know." The blind woman folded her arms and seemed to sleep.

A firm hand clasped Muluc's shoulder. Guards? She stiffened.

Balam looked down at the urchins. "Pretty expensive, don't you think?"

"I was just—"

"I traded the last pieces and came to help you with the sweets," he said. "Something smells good down this way."

The blind woman sat as still as the stone trees carved by the Lords' craftsmen, more a distant memory than a living person. Balam pulled Muluc's arm, taking the small jaguar from her hand.

"For me?" he asked.

"Yes," Muluc said, walking a few steps with Balam while looking back at the blind woman, who now rearranged her urchins on the mat. Had she imagined the whole thing?

"I like it," Balam said, slipping his arm around Muluc's waist.

Muluc enjoyed the warmth and weight of Balam's arm around her. Leaning her head against his shoulder, she inhaled the scent of coconut on his skin. She looked up into his eyes: warm with happiness. Desperately she wanted to feel the same way, but the blind woman's premonition echoed in her mind. How could she return to Cobá when it felt so far away and Balam felt so close? Balam squeezed her gently and rested his head on top of hers for a moment, making Muluc feel like liquid chocolate. Maybe she could send a messenger to her mother. Maybe Balam could come to Cobá. Or she could simply stay in Chichén. With those thoughts, the good feeling evaporated and Muluc pulled away from Balam's embrace.

"Something is wrong," he said. "Did that old woman frighten you?"

"She knows me," she whispered.

"She's just some old witch," Balam said. "I will protect you. I am fierce like the jaguar of my name." He held up the little yellow spotted carving and roared.

Even though her blood still tingled with lightning, Muluc laughed. Maybe if she ignored the bad feelings, they would go away.

She and Balam bought honey tortillas and gobbled them while walking arm in arm through the market, shopping for their feast.

. . .

"But I don't want to swim." Barb wouldn't budge from her seat when the bus stopped at the swimming cenote. "Let's skip it so you can finish the story."

Nando brushed back his dark hair. "I'm not like your American television telling you stories all day long."

"Nando's right. It's hot, and we should all go swimming," I said. This place looked a lot nicer than the swampy, but supposedly sacred, cenote. I rolled my swimsuit into my towel, glancing at Nando. He ignored me.

All the guys followed Monique off the bus. Max nudged Josh. Guess I wasn't the only one who'd seen Monique swimming back at the hotel.

"Just give me a hint," Barb begged. "One teeny tiny hint about Muluc."

"Leave him alone." I sighed and shook my head like Mom. Kind of satisfying, I must admit.

But just to spite me, Nando said in a low and menacing voice, "Cenote. Sacrifice."

"Oooh. I can't wait. I can't!"

"Come on." I whacked her with my towel. Very satisfying. This cenote was like a cave, but with stairs built down to the water. Fifty feet above us, sun glinted through the natural open-ing. Everyone climbed up to a ledge to jump into the water, except Barb, who swam off to hunt for lost treasure (Talia had left her precious Barbie to stalk Josh).

"Thousands of tourists have been here," I called after Barb. "Today!"

"So?" She treaded water. "I'm going to dive down deep. Over there, where the water is glittering like gold."

"That's sunlight."

Barb paddled into the middle of the cenote, where the sun shone and long vines reached into the water. I stood looking at the dark water, watching Barb dunk and dunk again. Why hadn't they installed lights? Were there rotting bones down there? Just standing in the cave felt nice and cool. Maybe I'd skip the whole swimming thing. Plus, who knew what kinds of creatures cruised around down there: strange, undiscovered prehistoric things with giant teeth. Plus, there might be an an-cient Mayan curse that doomed anyone who swam in a sacred cenote. Reason number—number teen something: ancient Mayan curses.

Josh pulled himself out of the water next to me. "Come on, Mountain Goat. It's your turn!" He grabbed my hand and led me up the stairs to the ledge. No boy had ever held my hand be-fore, not on purpose anyway. His hand felt wet but strong, not slippery, and totally electric. He looked down at me as we reached the highest jumping ledge. And C.C. looked at me with— envy! Talia and Nando both sent menacing looks my way.

Josh didn't seem to notice. "You're a daredevil, right? This is nothing."

I kind of nodded, completely unable to think of anything to say. When it was wet, Josh's hair looked even spikier than Zach B.'s. Josh had super-athletic legs. And he was actually flirting—with me!

"Let's go together, cutie." Josh bumped his hip against mine. "Ready: one, two, three!"

My face burned with such a deep, embarrassing blush that I had to jump before anyone saw; still holding hands, I pulled Josh after me, cannonballing into the water with a huge splash. Cold! How could the water be so cold when it was ninety degrees outside?

"That's a ten for splashibility," Max yelled.

"Nice jump," Luc said.

"Fun, huh?" Josh grinned at me, whipping his wet hair back from his face. I nodded like one of the bobblehead turtles Mom had bought Barb in the hotel gift shop.

"Give me a break." Talia wrung out her hair. "They jumped. What's the big deal?"

Nando watched me with wide eyes, kind of crinkling his forehead, but then Josh splashed me, and everyone else swam over for a huge water fight. I totally drenched Talia! At the end, all of the girls—except me—ganged up on Nando. Gemma got him good!

I paddled away, looking around for Barb, but I couldn't find her. Did some toothy beast snatch her, or did she drown chasing after an old soda can or something? While the others jumped off the ledge again, I swam over to the middle, keeping my legs close to the surface, although only the bravest creatures would stick around after all our splashing.

Monique (top on) and Dante treaded water while kissing near the vines. Barb bobbed up right next to me, so I shrieked. Dante and Monique laughed, so I splashed them.

"I found a gum wrapper and this!" Barb held up a small coin. "Ancient Mayan money."

"That's a peso."

"I know, but I can pretend." She swam away from me. "I'm going back under. Once your eyes adjust, the water's really clear."

I swam a few feet away so I wouldn't look like a perv, staring at Monique and Dante as they resumed kissing. From the highest ledge, Nando jumped into the water holding hands with Jessie and C.C. I felt a twinge of that old Zach B.-teasing-Fiona (in a flirty way) kind of jealousy, so I swam farther away, ignoring their echoing laughter. Why was he only mad at me? All of us made fun of his sacred swamp of a cenote. Not just me. And yeah, I climbed the pyramid, but it's not like millions of people hadn't done it before. I didn't hurt anything. And I kind of helped myself, I think.

I floated on my back and looked up at the opening at the top of the cavern, a stream of sunlight warming my face. Closing my eyes, I thought about the people sacrificed in the cenotes. How could the Mayans stand around and watch other people die? Why didn't someone try to stop them? Were their beliefs that strong? Or was it peer pressure? Sometimes the ancient Mayans seemed so cruel. Then again, people kill each other every day all over the world for no good reason. But we don't *sacrifice* each other. Or do we?

Grace Williams's face popped into my mind: puffy eyes, tears running down her cheeks.

"Please just tell me what 'pickle wart' means. Please?" she had begged.

I wanted to tell her. It was so stupid anyway—a dumb joke about a bumpy pickle and some guy Fiona had a crush on (and his you-know-what). Like Fiona even knew. Just as I was about to say something to Grace, Fiona glared at me, so I didn't say anything.

"Maybe you shouldn't have missed mini-camp," Fiona said.

"I had to visit my grandparents." Grace started sobbing.

While she cried, I stood there and watched the group sacrifice her. Would it be my turn this year? Did I care?

Yes.

When we got back on the bus, Nando seemed to be in a better mood; he almost sat in the back with C.C., but Barb begged for "just a little more of the story."

I headed back to sit with Josh, but Barb pulled me into her seat. "Kat needs to listen too."

Nando scoffed. "She doesn't care. To her, Mexico is all about swimming. Getting a tan."

I rolled my eyes. This guy really etched his grudges into stone.

"But Kat *loves* your story." Barb pulled *my* travel journal out of *my* backpack. "She's always drawing pictures about it and everything." Before I could snatch *my* journal back, the pages flipped open to a drawing of how I imagined Snake. Nando tilted his head to see it, but I snapped the book closed, whacking it against Barb's arm—hard—before shoving it deep into my backpack.

"Little brat of a traitor!" I growled.

Barb squirmed away from me and slipped into Nando's seat. But Nando didn't acknowledge her, still staring at me, his forehead furrowed. "Okay, I'll tell you about the rain ceremony," he said, looking at me the way I'd stared at those complicated Mayan carvings, trying to figure out what was there.

• • •

THE DAY 4 BEN
Protector of Growing Corn

Muluc felt as if she were swimming through the bodies flooding the Great Plaza on the day of the Lords' rain ceremony. Thousands of men, women, and children crowded between the temples, each vying for the best view. Balam weaved through the crowd, as agile as a jungle cat racing through thick underbrush. Macaw and Mol went to stake out a place near the Temple of the Warriors to see the end of the ceremony, but Balam wanted Muluc to see everything. Holding hands, they twisted through the crowd toward the Temple of the Jaguars to see the ball-game procession.

The hot sun and crush of bodies made Muluc dizzy as they stood waiting all afternoon; the smell of sweat mixed with the sweet clouds of pom incense nauseated her. She'd eaten so much during their feast last night that she worried she might get sick. Leaning against Balam's shoulder, she sipped water from a small gourd he had brought. Muluc had never attended a ceremony as a commoner— she had always sat, wearing newly embroidered clothing, with the elites. Smoothing her plain white cotton dress made her long for her old status in Cobá. She licked her finger and rubbed a bit of spit on her lip plug to make the stone shine.

Priests, wearing cloth woven with red for blood and blue for sacrifice, climbed the steps to the high chamber in the Temple of the Jaguars that over-looked the ball court. Balam told Muluc that they sat at a table held up by small statues of a dozen men representing all the different priest classes at Chichén. Dishes piled high with exotic foods for the gods covered the table.

Muluc stood on her tippy-toes, craning her neck. "I wish I could see it!"

"Just wait until you see the ballplayers," Balam said.

Musicians standing along the top of the high stone walls played long wooden trumpets, rattles, flutes, and conch shells and beat turtle drums with deer antlers. Like trees blowing in the wind, the entire crowd moved to the rhythm of the music. Muluc closed her eyes, absorbing the drumbeat as

Balam put his hands on her hips. The music grew louder, and royal guards parted the crowd.

A Lord dressed in a cape of thousands of shimmering green quetzal feathers walked to the temple. The crowd hushed as he climbed the narrow stairway, but the musicians rapidly beat their drums. With his feathered cape glittering in the afternoon sun, the Lord sat on the red jaguar throne between two columns, each one carved with creation gods standing on Snake Mountain.

Muluc peeked over people's heads and looked at the mural on the wall of the temple, trembling at the sight of the losing ballplayer falling back against a ball, a stream of blood shaped like a snake shooting out from his neck while the victorious ballplayer hovered over him. Lower down on the mural, warriors cared for another dead body.

"The Lord makes my skin prickle too, sometimes." Balam rubbed Muluc's arms. "Wait until you see the warriors."

Saying nothing, Muluc sipped some warm water, trying to swallow her fear as well. Why hadn't she stayed back in the jungle, safe in Macaw's hut?

Balam pulled Muluc closer to the procession, where men blowing conch shells led the parade. An old priest carrying a small offering bowl followed behind. Shouts rose as the ballplayers strode past wearing headdresses with layers of colorful feathers. On their chests they wore wooden yokes, carved with images of the gods, over thick padding to protect their bodies from the heavy rubber ball. Thick leather skirts covered their groins. Padding also wound around their forearms. Some carried small carved handstones for hitting the ball. The warriors' backs glittered with tiny mirrors as they entered the ball court.

A large man, damp with sweat and smelling of fermented corn, crushed Muluc's foot as he tried to get a closer look. She cried out, but no one heard her. Even Balam cheered so loud that Muluc covered her ears, as a warrior, wearing an elaborate headdress of quetzal feathers, ended the procession of ballplayers. The warrior's skirt flamed with a huge red-feathered snake emerging from a tortoise's shell, and he wore a glittering yoke studded with gems and carved with symbols of Kulkucan, the Great Vision Serpent. Muluc's whole body went cold. She edged backwards, but Balam held her.

"He's the greatest warrior in all of Chichén!" Balam shouted. "The great Kan!"

"Snake," Muluc whispered.

Snake gazed into a gold mirror in his hand, as if he were a sorcerer peering into the Otherworld.

"He has great powers—like a priest," Balam said, not taking his eyes off Snake.

Muluc tried to hide her face in Balam's neck, but he shrugged her off.

"Watch," he said.

Muluc looked up just as Snake stood next to them. In spite of the heat, she shivered. Snake glanced over; his eyes met hers and widened; his mouth curved upward into a leering grin. He raised his mirror, and the crowd cheered. Muluc leaned against Balam.

"I feel dizzy," she said.

"Kan has that effect on girls," Balam teased, handing her the water gourd. "Let's head over to the show." Balam pulled her through the waves of people. "Why are your hands so cold?"

Looking back, Muluc saw Parrot Nose's—no, Quetzal's—brother, dressed as a ballplayer. Did he have a chance against Snake? Her breath caught as she also saw the bloody image on the mural—painted with so much red.

Balam bumped through the mass of bodies, making his way to the small platform near the temple of Kulkucan. "Hurry," he said. "They've already started."

Muluc held Balam's hand, allowing him to lead her like a child, no longer wanting to even glimpse bits of the ball game. Would Quetzal ever know his brother's fate? Who would tell him?

Cheers from the royal crowd watching the ball game erupted over the noises of the commoners in the plaza. The elites chanted, "Kan! Kan! Kan!" Snake. Muluc felt the lightning in her blood that quickened her step, even though her foot still throbbed. If only she could run from the plaza and find a quiet place in the jungle. No longer like one kernel of corn in a whole field, she'd been recognized. But she couldn't bring herself to tear her hand from Balam's.

They stopped near the front of a small stage where performers dressed in warrior costumes tossed corn into the crowd.

"Do you know the Hero Twins story?" Balam asked.

Muluc nodded.

"I love this part," Balam said. "Where the Lords of Death challenge the Hero Twins to a ball game in Xibalba."

"Hurrah!" people in the crowd yelled as the actors drank pulque and then spit it out into the crowd. A few drops of the sweet-smelling liquid landed on Muluc's hand. Rather than wipe it off on her clean dress, Muluc stuck her fingers into her mouth. The smoky, peppery pulque prickled her tongue. Balam laughed at the expression on her face, then drew her close, folding her into the curve of his body, making her forget Snake. Losing herself in Balam's affection, Muluc only half watched the familiar story unfolding onstage. Again and again the Hero Twins tricked the Lords of Death, escaping the Razor House, the Cold House, the Jaguar

House. Could Muluc ever be so clever? She hadn't even *tried* to escape her enslavement in Chichén. And now Snake had seen her!

Children dressed as fierce bats swarmed the stage as the Hero Twins spent the night in Bat House. "Eeek, eeek, eeek," they squealed.

"Come on, let's go," Balam said. "Let's find my mother and Mol."

"But I love the part when the boys are burned, thrown into the river, and return alive three days later." Muluc stopped walking. "Can't we stay?" She did not want to go anywhere near the warriors. Snake. Could he steal her again? Or worse?

"Let's go. Trust me," Balam said.

Somehow Balam found Macaw, who had secured a spot close to the Temple of the Warriors. Muluc looked up the long flight of stairs at the Chac Mool statue reclining between two great pillars of Vision Serpents whose red mouths gaped open onto the platform on either side of him. Images of jaguars and eagles devouring hearts, as well as other ritual scenes, covered the temple—nothing like the staid depictions of royal families at Cobá. Then Muluc remembered the carving of Cobá's queen standing above a group of prisoners. Did they represent actual people like Quetzal's brother? Like herself? Would Balam be treated like a prisoner in Cobá? A shiver ran through her body.

Heat radiated from the stone buildings as

everyone waited for the biggest part of the ceremony. Muluc's head ached, and she longed to rest in the shade, but the ball game went on and on. The intense sunlight hurt her eyes; the sound of squalling babies exploded in her ears; and the smell of sweaty bodies and incense made her queasy. She felt a little better after drinking the sweet coconut milk Balam brought her, and Macaw insisted that she eat a few tortillas as well.

As the sun slid toward the Otherworld, cooling shadows crept across the plaza, yet the ball game continued. The throng grew quiet but restless. Men dressed as monkeys roamed among the crowd, dancing, playing tricks on people, taking their food, mimicking them, making them laugh. One came and put a tortilla on Mol's head, and Balam laughed so hard he tipped over backwards. Muluc tried to help him sit up again, but he pulled her down next to him. A cottony cloud stretched across the sky as Muluc and Balam, lying next to each other, held hands.

At last, as the sun disappeared behind the trees, a final cheer roared from the ball court.

"It's time," Balam whispered to Muluc, brushing his lips against her ear.

Sitting up, Muluc looked behind her and watched a procession part the crowd. People stood, but they did not cheer. Mothers quieted their children, reminding them to be respectful. The warriors came first, battle weary. Muluc saw Snake, but he did not search the crowd. He wore a somber expression and walked with a heavy step; still, Muluc felt like she couldn't take a deep breath, as if heavy stones pressed against her chest. Her heart pulsed in her stomach as the warriors climbed the steep stairway and flanked the platform. From the small doorway, the Lords of Chichén emerged, but the crowd remained quiet.

Balam stared straight ahead.

Resembling extravagant jungle birds, the Lords wore long, fluttering feathered capes, headdresses, and loincloths. Girls came out and spread white cloths at the feet of the Lords while servants carried out trays. Lifting long stingray spines from the tray, the Lords each pulled their loincloths away from their bodies and pierced their privates so that blood dripped onto the white cloths below. The servants collected the cloths, placed them in a large bowl in front of the Chac Mool statue, and dipped a torch to the fabric, lighting it in flame. Just like the Hero Twins' bodies. Muluc watched the smoke drift into the sky to feed the gods.

Next, the royal women appeared, wearing elaborate embroidery, their limbs heavy with jewelry. Servants spread more cloth and carried trays with slender vine ropes. The queens knelt on the white cloths while more servants appeared with goblets, from which the women drank. Then the queens pulled the vine ropes through their tongues, spilling their blood in sacrifice to the gods. Again the servants burned the cloth.

Warriors emerged from the small room between the snake pillars, leading two men who were naked but painted with thick blue dye, and presented them to the Lords. The Lords sprinkled the captives with the ashes of their blood sacrifice. Then the captives drank from a cup.

People cheered when Snake presented the captives to the crowd.

"Sons from the kingdom of Cobá, you have been defeated on the Great Ball Court of Chichén," Snake called out.

Balam raised his fist and shouted along with everyone else.

As she tried to discern the features of the men through the thick blue paint, fear exploded into Muluc's heart like thunder breaking into a burst of rain. Quetzal's brother was the taller one. Her head pounded in rhythm with her heart. The men stumbled as the drink numbed them, but the warriors held them standing.

The Lords began uttering a prayer to the gods, hushing the crowd again. Priests entered the stairway from the hallway below, chanting a song to the gods of rain and maize as small boys scattered corn kernels on the steps of the temple.

A servant appeared, carrying a long knife across

his open palms. The warriors took the shorter captive and lay him across the Chac Mool. Then a priest dressed in a cape of blue feathers raised the knife and plunged it deep into the captive's flesh. Red blood ran in purple rivulets as it mixed with the blue paint. The priest worked quickly, lifting the man's heart to the sky.

Fear roared through her body, but Muluc could not look away. Warriors lifted the man's lifeless form and tossed him down the stairs, as if into the Otherworld. As the priest placed the heart in the dish held by the Chac Mool statue, Muluc focused on Quetzal's brother. His eyes had closed, and two warriors supported the weight of his body as they led him to be sacrificed.

Muluc tugged Balam's hand. Briefly their eyes met. Muluc tried to speak. Couldn't. Balam wrinkled his forehead.

"What?" he asked.

Muluc's mouth felt tight and small.

"Come on," Balam whispered.

Muluc allowed him to lead her away—she did not want to see more here. She wanted to return to the jungle and cry until her sleeping mat looked like it had been left in the rain. If only she could wrap herself in her mother's arms and weep like a child with a skinned knee.

With the crowd crushing against them, Balam

led Muluc to the white road running from the Great Plaza past gardens wilted from lack of water. Why weren't they heading back into the jungle? The road reminded Muluc of the great white roads radiating from Cobá, and she began to cry, filling her mouth with the taste of her salty tears. Balam didn't notice as he pushed Muluc through the people clogging the road until they reached the edge of a deep cenote. Sheer rock walls surrounded a huge pool of water shimmering dark green in the dusky light—the portal to Xibalba. More priests and warriors led a group of men, women, and children, all painted blue, toward the cenote.

"From Cobá?" Muluc asked with a squeaky voice.

"Most from Chichén," Balam said. "It's a great honor to be wanted by the gods and a good way for the poor to win the gods' favor."

Muluc looked down at the deep green pool. What would the cool water feel like? How would it feel to be embraced by the gods? She stepped closer. Closer. Balam pulled her back. The priests chanted prayers and gave the sacrificial victims long drinks from a painted vessel. The potion acted quickly. One small girl fell to the ground, and the priest lifted her in his arms, like a father picking up an injured child, but then he tossed her into the cenote, where she landed with a soft splash.

"We will see you in three days," he called.

Like the Hero Twins. One by one the others fell into the cenote.

"Do they really emerge again?" Muluc asked as the bodies began to sink.

"Sometimes, but usually as newborn souls," Balam said. "In rich royal families."

People came forward to make their own offerings: clay figures, corn, incense, pottery, wooden statues—all the things that feed the gods. Balam threw in one of Muluc's best figures of Chac.

"Sure to bring rain," he told Muluc.

Muluc took a stone out of her earlobe and tossed it into the cenote to ensure that Quetzal's brother would return to life. A good life.

As night fell dark, the plaza drained of people. In the sky, the Great Vision Serpent loomed over the ball court. Muluc held Balam's hand tight as they walked the long dark road home. A single cloud obscured the moon.

• • •

CHAPTER EIGHT

Hi! I climbed this pyramid today (even though I kind of wasn't supposed to—guess I'm turning into a rebel. LOL). All the guys nicknamed me Mountain Goat.

Swam in a gorgeous cenote (75 feet down). Long jungly vines hung into the water. So exotic! The guys are all definite tens! Must be a requirement to get in the country.

Barb is driving me crazy with her treasure hunting!

Love, Kat

. . .

I wiped the steam off the bathroom mirror and squeezed a blackhead on my chin.

"Kat, get out of there." Barb pounded on the door. "I have to get ready too!"

"Go use Mom and Dad's."

"I'm not going in there."

"It's been cleaned," I said.

"You said it wasn't clean enough for you," Barb said. "So it's not clean enough for me either."

Fine. I opened the door. Barb ran in and turned on the shower.

"What do you think Muluc will do next? I can't believe we have to wait two more days."

"I really don't care," I said.

"You do too," Barb said. "I saw you listening, and then I totally saw you drawing. So there!" She stepped into the marble shower. "Do you think Nando is still mad at you? What if he doesn't want us to come to his sister's party now? You should have never, ever—"

"Shut up," I said. "What you should have never, ever done was show him my journal. And I don't even care about the stupid party. Nando obviously hates me."

"He does not. I think he likes you. Not *like,* like, you know, because of that pretty girl at lunch, but—"

"Whatever." I left the bathroom, turning off the lights just long enough to make Barb scream, before flicking them back on again. "I totally don't care."

I flopped on the bed. Truth? I couldn't stop thinking of Nando and the girl at lunch. After swimming, we'd gone to this restaurant a few miles away. Barb stalked Nando all the way to a table near the back, hoping to hear another installment in "Days of Muluc's Life." Max and Josh invited me to sit with them, but then Talia brushed past me, dragging Luc along, and stole my seat, so I sat next to Barb and Nando. While

Barb unsuccessfully nagged Nando, I pulled out my journal and added reason number 50: Talia, Talia, Talia!

Nando leaned over to look at my notebook. "Are you drawing?"

"Not exactly."

"I liked the drawing of Snake," Nando said. "He looked just like I imagined him in my mind too."

Before I could think of anything to say or even process the fact that Nando was being nice to me, even after my pyramid climb, he completely turned his back to me.

Great, I thought. *I've blown it yet again.* But then I followed his gaze across the room to the gorgeous Mayan girl taking orders and laughing at Josh's jokes. Nando's shoulders tensed, and he wouldn't take his eyes off the girl, even when I spilled my ice water and stole his napkin to wipe it up. When the girl came to our table and smiled her perfect white teeth smile and said something in Mayan, Nando acted goofy. And I felt, well—I felt jealous, I guess. And then I felt stupid. After all, he was Mayan, I was American, and my friends wouldn't even give him a good score—just points for breathing. Plus, he hates Americans. And he didn't exactly think much of me anyway, except he apparently liked my sketches. Whatever. The guy would still toss me into that creepy cenote without a second thought.

While we ate tortillas and chicken, all the waitresses did a Mayan dance. Nando's girl danced right in front of us, doing complicated footwork with an open, full bottle of Coke on her head, and she didn't spill one drop. Pretty impressive, even though it was a little wacky. Nando stared at her as if it were the best thing he'd ever seen. Barb nudged me and smiled her all-knowing nine-year-old smile. Such a child! But the girl was completely pretty: great figure, smooth brown skin (not a single blackhead), silky black hair with a red flower tucked behind one ear. I wondered if she'd be at the stupid birthday party too, along with Alfredo's great love—if we were still invited after I practically ruined Chichén Itzá and everything.

To take my mind off Nando, I sat on the bed and opened my journal and sketched the cenote, writing a few notes about how the cold water felt, how Josh's hand felt. But I kept seeing Nando laughing with the cheerleaders, Nando staring googly-eyed at the beautiful waitress, so I sketched her too.

"What are you daydreaming about?" Barb asked now, combing her wet hair. "Hurry, so we can go get dinner. I'm starving."

Mom knocked on the door. "Come on, girls; we're ready." She walked in wearing a short red sundress that showed off her new tan. Mom was having my ideal vacation!

"Just a minute." I hopped up, still wearing my towel, and searched through my suitcase.

"You've been back for an hour," Mom said. "What's taking so long?"

"Maybe I'm tired," I said. "We drove like a million miles into the jungle today."

What time *was* it? Looking out the window at the darkening

sky, I realized that I hadn't thought of Fiona at four p.m. Oh well. I'm sure she wasn't thinking of me either.

"Wear a dress." Mom sighed and shook her head. "We're going to the seafood restaurant."

"Barb threw her stupid wet swimsuit into my suitcase." I held up a babyish watermelon sundress Mom had bought during one of her many shopping excursions in the hotel gift shop (reason number 49). "And this is all I have left," I said. "I'm *not* about to wear it."

"Then you can skip dinner," Mom said.

I grimaced at the silly dress. "Fine. But no little happy family memory photos."

"Oh, that reminds me," Mom said. "We're having dinner with one of the girls on your tour."

"What?" I asked.

"Who?" Barb asked.

"I think her name is Tanya. She's from Omaha. Mother just got divorced," Mom said. "Sad situation. Tanya's had a lot of trouble this past year."

"Wrong tour," I said. "That figures. You go hook up with someone on the wrong tour." I shook my head and sighed a gigantic sigh.

"We don't have a Tanya on our tour," Barb said.

"Well, we're having dinner with Tanya and her mother." Mom walked out of the room. "Our reservation is in fifteen minutes, so step on it," she called back to us.

I frantically searched through my suitcase for something else to wear, but Barb's dumb swimsuit had oozed on everything decent. I was stuck with little red watermelons. New reason number—Oh, never mind. I slipped the dress over my head and whacked Barb in the arm for laughing at me.

An old wooden fishing boat decorated the restaurant entrance, and fishing nets hung from the ceiling. In the far corner I saw Talia's blue-blond hair hanging over the back of a wooden chair.

"Please don't let us sit by them," I said.

"What was that?" Dad asked.

"Nothing."

"Cheer up," he said. "That dress looks great on you."

"I look like a two-year-old who needs to wear training pants."

Ignored.

"There they are." Mom waved at Talia's table, and a woman with short blond hair waved back.

"Mom probably got her name wrong," Barb said.

"But Omaha? Talia goes on and on about New York."

"Talia told me about Omaha," Barb said.

"Yeah, she's your great buddy. Whatever. I'd rather have room service."

We sat down at the table, and Talia glanced at my watermelon dress, then read her menu like it was the last chapter of an incredible novel, even though Barb asked her a million questions.

Mom transformed into cheery hostess mode. "Julie," she announced, "these are my daughters, Barbara and Katherine." Mom smiled at Julie. "We met that first day waiting for your bus to return."

"And that's when the fun really started!" Julie and Mom giggled like they had their own inside joke. Whatever. Then Julie leaned toward Barb. "Tanya told me she wishes she had a little sister just like you." Julie sighed. "Wasn't meant to be."

Talia glanced at me for just a second. Was she actually jealous of me? Because I had an annoying little sister? No way. Not possible. Right?

Barb started rambling. "She's been so nice to me. Once, she helped me find shells. Another time—"

Julie smiled at Barb, and even Talia-Tanya seemed to smile.

Julie turned to me. "Have you been enjoying the tour?"

"It's okay," I said.

"I love it!" Barb exclaimed. "We've seen—"

Mom gave Barb the hush sign with her finger. Does she even know what I've been going through for the last few days?

"I feel like I'm in another world here," Julie said. "The sun, the beach, the beautiful blue water." She smiled. "I sure have needed the relaxation."

"I bet it's nothing like New York," I said.

"You must mean Omaha, dear," Julie said.

"I thought Talia—Tanya—was from New York," I said.

Julie glanced at Tanya, sighing and shaking her head. Do all mothers do that?

"Tanya's father recently moved to upstate New York, but she hasn't visited him yet."

Tanya put down her menu and looked at me with wide eyes. Waiting. I didn't say a word. I wasn't going to be that kind of person. That would be beneath *me*.

"Can I still call you Talia?" Barb whispered. "I love that

name, and I've already changed my stuffed dolphin's name from Aqua to Talia."

Tanya nodded.

Our parents chatted like best friends for the rest of the dinner—like, seriously, they'd known each other for what, four days? Dad went on and on about going deep-sea fishing, and Mom invited Julie to go snorkeling. Tanya only pushed her shrimp linguine around her plate, but I enjoyed every bite of my tuna steak so much that I even stopped feeling stupid in my watermelon dress. I remembered what Nando said about Tanya's teasing: "You don't have anything to lose by standing up for yourself, but you can lose yourself by trying to please everyone." Calling Tanya on her lies felt good, and kind of bad. Anyway, I didn't need to have her like me. Let her and Barb have their little fake sister club. She could hate me all she wants. It wasn't like Fiona and everyone at home. Was it?

After dinner Dad and Mom stopped by the concierge to make "romantic" dinner reservations for the next night. Turns out Barb and I *were* still invited to the big fifteenth-birthday party. Dad had apparently gotten all the details from Alfredo when the bus dropped us off.

While Mom and Dad debated beachfront dining versus gourmet Mayan food in town, I watched one of the maids, down on her hands and knees, polishing the marble floor. I couldn't help but think about Muluc—she'd gone from living in a palace with marble floors to a hut with dirt floors. What kind of house did the maid live in? I looked at the lobby clock. It was almost ten o'clock at night. Did she have children at home? Nando had talked about how they couldn't grow everything they needed anymore, but I hadn't thought about how the people working at the resorts were probably Mayan. The maid wiped her forehead. Did she hate tourists too? I suddenly felt guilty for leaving my wet towels on the floor "for the maid to pick up."

I was feeling a confusion of emotions as we walked back to our room. The resort looked so perfect compared with the little villages we passed through on the way to Chichén Itzá. So I wasn't in the mood for Barb's "superduper" excitement about Nando's sister's party. "What should I wear? Should I bring my swimsuit? My stuffed dolphin? Oh, and I can't forget—"

I wanted to forget about everything. "I don't know," I said. "Staying all night in some strange jungle village?" I pulled at a loose thread in my dress. "It's not like we really know these people."

Barb danced around the room, unable to contain herself. Super.

"Honey, I've trusted them to drive you all over the jungle this whole past week," Mom said, kicking off her shoes. "I hardly think this is the time to worry, and this was always part of the plan."

"But this could be part of their plan—they could be thieving, kidnapping bandits, like I wrote on my list. Numbers—" My list of reasons sounded so stupid all of a sudden.

"Kat, really," Mom said.

"Besides, no one would want to kidnap you, Kat," Barb said. "Trust me."

"Oh yeah? And you're such a prize," I said.

"I don't think you need to worry," Dad said. "Paul considers the Eks family."

"So we're like cousins?" Barb asked.

"Hardly," I said. Sure, Nando seemed to kind of forgive me for climbing that pyramid, but what if he was just waiting to seek revenge? New reason number— Oh, never mind.

"Mom, don't listen to Kat. I want to see Nando's village," Barb said.

"Then you go. I'll stay here." I thought about all the dangerous things on my list, even if it was a stupid list: jaguars, poisonous plants, monkeys with Ebola virus, dengue fever . . .

"It's going to be very educational," Dad said. "I'd love to spend time in a real Mayan village."

"So, why don't *you* go?"

"We've got plans." Dad walked behind Mom and kissed her neck. "A romantic candlelight dinner to start."

"Remember, tomorrow's our actual anniversary." Mom kissed Dad again.

"Not in front of the children," I said.

Squealing and clapping, Barb jumped up and down on the bed until Mom made her stop. Oh, how these people make me suffer. Maybe I *would* rather brave a night in a strange village. Couldn't be too much worse than spending time with my own family. But would I have to sleep on a dirt floor?

CHAPTER NINE

Tour buses zoomed past us like rockets as Dad merged onto the highway that led to Nando's mysterious dirt road. The car hiccupped and coughed as Dad pressed down on the accelerator.

"Dad, you're driving like a little old lady," I said.

He shuddered and gripped the steering wheel. "This isn't exactly a Ferrari."

"Well, you need to keep up, or we'll get squashed like bugs." A truck blasted its horn before passing us on the dirt shoulder. I'd survived a week on these roads, and now I was going to die.

"I think I'm getting too old for this." Dad slammed his foot down on the gas pedal, and the car rumbled down the road, shaking. "I'm beginning to remember why we traded in that old yellow Bug."

"You should see how fast the tour bus goes," Barb said.

I hung on to the little handle on the dashboard as if it were some kind of safety bar. A simple seat belt would make me feel much better about this situation. I tried not to crush the little wrapped package in my hand; Mom had picked out some silver-and-turquoise earrings shaped like turtles for Nando's sister. What if she hates turtles?

"We're getting close." I pointed down the road. "It's the next road after that grass-roofed hut thing."

Nando was waiting for us when we pulled over. I stepped out of the car and looked past him at the narrow road disappearing into the thick trees—just the kind of road where Muluc got kidnapped. But I'd made a decision; I would forget my list of fears and be brave. I took a deep breath and counted to ten. Yup, brave. Tugging our backpacks, Barb climbed out of the back seat.

"Here we go, I guess." I gave Dad a small wave.

"Wait," Dad said. "I want to drive you to the village and meet Señor Ek."

"You can't, Dad," said Barb. "Cars can't go on Nando's road."

"You're kidding me," Dad said.

"The road is really rocky," Barb said.

"Limestone," I said, using Dad's own encyclopedia voice.

"I seem to remember that we did walk to several cenotes when I came here with Paul." Dad looked down the path that led into the jungle. "You have to promise me—"

"We'll be safe." I hope. "You'll remember how to get back here, Dad?"

Nando walked over to the car, and Dad got out.

"So nice to meet you, Señor." Nando shook Dad's hand. "Don't worry. My family will take good care of Kat and Barb."

Dad looked a little more relaxed. Nando's great smile. They talked for a few minutes while I scanned the jungle, looking for any signs of danger.

"Bye, Daddy." Barb hugged Dad. "Thanks a bunch."

We started to walk down the bumpy road to Nando's house

as Dad got back in the car and watched us. I stumbled in a rocky place and heard Dad honk three times, so I waved my hand over my head without turning around. Maybe this was a big mistake.

"Your father is very nice," Nando said.

"He's the greatest," Barb gushed, and gave far too many examples of Dad's so-called greatness. The kid doesn't know when to shut up.

I didn't contribute a word to Barb's little Dad-fest. Ahead, the road curved, so we could no longer see the highway, and a few moments later we heard the old car rumble to a start. Hidden in all those trees, I felt like we were a million miles away from civilization. Even in the shade the air felt hot and thick and smelled heavy with damp leaves; birds called to each other in the canopy of trees. The muddy path narrowed, and we walked single file.

I stopped, taking a deep breath, resting my hand on the trunk of a tree. Crisscross marks had been slashed into the bark all the way up. "Who had it in for this tree?"

"That's the chewing gum tree, the zapote," he said.

I looked at all the marks. "You don't chew the tree, do you?"

Nando smirked. "No, you chew the sap. And you cut the tree to get the sap."

His look said it all: I'd scored another zero in intelligence.

"How did they get all the way up there?" I asked.

"Ropes," Nando said. "It was very dangerous and slippery work. The sap flows best when it rains."

"So the sap runs out of the slash marks?" Barb asked.

"*Sí*. They collected it in big heavy sacks. Many of my great uncles worked as *chicleros*," he said. "The stories they told . . ."

"Stories?" Barb asked. Seriously, the kid needs help. Professional help.

"About the *banditos* who hid in the *chiclero* camps," Nando said. "No one used to come to this part of the Yucatán — until they built Cancún."

"Bet you would have loved it back then," I said.

Nando frowned. "Life was hard."

"But there weren't any tourists." I started walking again, adding a little sway to my hips.

"Bandits were worse — but just a little bit," Nando teased.

"Yeah, I bet they climbed all over your precious pyramids with their dirty feet."

"Kat." Nando shook his head. "You are like a jaguar cub, always hissing and snarling for a fight."

What? That's totally not true. I couldn't help it if people — like Talia — always picked on me. He should see me with Fiona: I was an obedient dog. Ooh. That sounds bad. I mean I was a loyal friend, like a dog. Whatever.

"Forget about her," Barb said. "What did the bandits do?"

"Bad things," Nando said. "Sometimes honest men would work all season collecting the sticky sap, boiling it, and forming it into blocks for the big chewing gum factories in the United States, only to be robbed or killed on their way out of the jungle."

"That's so mean," Barb said.

We walked in silence for several minutes. Leaves rustled on the side of the path, so I turned quickly to look. An iguana scurried up a tree trunk, but my heart raced as I imagined being stalked by some outlaw who would hold me and Barb for ransom. I took a deep breath, trying to enjoy the quiet. Trying not to think. Again Nando stopped. He pointed to bouncing branches in the trees high above.

"Howler monkeys," he said.

"Are they your pets?" Barb asked.

"No," Nando said. "They are wild." The monkeys looked down at us.

"They're watching us," I said. Like trained spies.

"A whole family of howler monkeys lives near my village," Nando said. "Spider monkeys too."

"They're so cute," Barb said as the monkeys hopped to another tree.

About a half-hour later we arrived at a cluster of thatched-roof huts in Nando's village. I felt strange, like I'd stepped into Muluc's story: the houses were made of thin tree trunks tied together with twine, leaving gaps in the walls, and they had short rock walls surrounding them. A couple of huts had been painted bright turquoise blue, but the rest looked like they hadn't made it past the dead-trees-strapped-together phase. In the distance I saw a lake shimmering in the sunlight.

"You live near a lake?" I asked.

"It's a cenote."

"It doesn't look like that other cenote we swam in," Barb said.

"This one is on the surface," he said. "But we have another one in our village too. I'll show it to you later."

Nando stopped in front of a large oval hut. "Here is my home." A sleeping dog raised his head to greet us. Through two open doorways, I could see the lake.

"You live right on the water," Barb said.

Fiona's patio umbrellas looked sturdier than Nando's so-called house.

"It's our air conditioner," Nando said. "We build our homes with two doors so the breeze flows through. That is also why we leave gaps in our walls. Plus, you can see out, and no one can see in."

Barb waved to the outside wall.

"Hola," someone said.

Barb put her hand down really fast, and I laughed.

"Come in and meet my mama," Nando said.

We entered the cool, dark hut. A young girl swung in a hammock, and other hammocks hung on small wooden hooks. In one corner stood a low wooden table, an old-fashioned grinding stone, a place for a fire on the floor, and some jars. I had no idea that Nando's family was so poor. The floor *was* made of dirt!

"This is *mi prima,* Maria." Nando tilted his head toward his cousin. "Maria, this is Kat and Barb."

"Señor Paul's *amigas! ¡Hola!*"

Barb set her backpack right down, but I held on to mine. Nando watched me.

He shrugged, blushing. "It's not like your American houses, but—"

"It's really cozy, though," Barb said.

We *would* have to sleep in the dirt with the bugs and who knows what other creepy crawlies. Why didn't Mom let me have a cell phone? I can't believe she made us do this! We were trapped out here! I reluctantly set my backpack next to Barb's, knowing I'd have to check it later.

"Is this your kitchen?" Barb asked. "Oh, is this where your mom made those tortillas? Will she make some for us?"

I didn't see a sink. How did they wash anything? Everything looked clean. But still. I didn't plan to eat anything. Not until we got back to civilization.

"Just wait until you see the feast for Isabel's *quinceañera,*" Nando said. "I hope you are hungry."

No way would I be hungry. Not until tomorrow. At the hotel buffet.

Nando spoke to Maria in Mayan.

"*Mi mamá* is helping Isabel get ready," he said. "We could go for a canoe ride?"

"That sounds great," Barb said.

"I don't know," I said. "Me and paddling . . ."

"Come on," Nando said. "We only have crocodiles in the water here."

Only crocodiles. Weren't they one of the reasons on my list? Whatever. I know I'd read something terrible about them anyway. Something involving lost limbs, death . . .

"Crocodiles!" Barb squealed. "I've never seen a real crocodile before. We only have alligators at our zoo. Are they your pets?"

"Americans!" Nando shook his head, but this time he smiled.

The canoe wobbled as I stepped into it, and I was sure I was going to fall in and become a crocodile snack.

Nando pointed to a spot where the water rippled across the lake. "Crocodile."

"Hurry!" Barb started to paddle.

"You want to paddle too?" Nando asked me.

"I don't think so." I looked down into the murky water. Reminded me of the sacrifice cenote—definitely not for drinking. Would Nando toss us to the crocodile god or something?

"He disappeared." Barb sounded so disappointed.

"I can find one." Nando paddled over to the tall reeds growing at the edge of the lake. Sure enough, there was a crocodile lounging in the shallow water, still as a log. One eye watched us.

"Do people in your village ever get attacked by crocodiles?" Barb asked.

"Just when we sacrifice foreign captives," Nando said.

I took a deep breath. "What kind of ceremony are we attending tonight?"

"Don't look so worried," Nando said. "Mayans don't do that kind of sacrifice anymore. Now we make offerings like liquor, food, incense—that kind of thing."

I wasn't so sure. Maybe trying to be brave was a stupid idea. Back to the list: crocodiles were reason number 10. And reason number 7 was sacrifice.

"Tell us about your sister's party," Barb said.

"When girls turn fifteen, it's an ancient tradition to have a special ceremony and a feast to celebrate that they are now women, not girls," Nando said. "Girls used to get married at fifteen, but now most finish school first." Nando handed me the paddle. "You paddle us back."

I shook my head.

"Come on, you can do it," he said. "It's easier than climbing El Castillo."

I smirked at him and shook my head. "No thanks." Then again, the paddle might make a good weapon if Nando tried anything sneaky. "Okay, I guess." Pressing the paddle into the water, I stroked, pulling the paddle back hard.

I bumped into the crocodile.

Barb and Nando laughed so hard that the boat started rocking like crazy. I gripped the sides until my knuckles turned white. The crocodile closed his eyes, rating me a complete zero.

Not even worth attacking.

Just before sunset we walked a narrow path through the trees to the little village church for Isabel's *quinceañera* ceremony. On a long table in the front of the church stood small statues of Catholic saints covered with colorful clothes, flowers piled at their feet. Three green crosses hung on the wall. Wearing dresses and necklaces! This was not like anything I'd seen that one time I went to Mass with Fiona. Smoke from burning incense sweetened the air as the ceremony started.

Isabel stood in front of the altar. She wore a pink dress like Fiona's sister had worn to prom. She had short curled hair, small earrings, high-heeled shoes, and gloves like a woman in an old movie. Seven girls wearing blue dresses stood on one side of her and seven boys wearing dark pants and white shirts stood on the other. All the girls wore crowns of flowers in their hair and looked so beautiful and grown-up. I recognized one girl—the dancer Nando liked at lunch the other day. She looked even prettier today, with her silky hair swept up into a bun.

The priest spoke Spanish so fast I couldn't understand a word, so I looked around and noticed Alfredo sitting in the row behind Nando and his family. People packed into the tiny church, crowding every single space. Barb and I sat in the back on the last row of benches, and even though people made a big deal about us being "Señor Paul's *amigas*," I felt white. Very, very white. Every person who walked through the door gawked at us.

The ceremony droned on.

The little chapel felt like a sauna: incense, sweat, heat. Some men left their seats and stood in the doorway, smoking. My head got dizzy. I wished I hadn't come. I didn't belong here.

A baby crawled over, pulled herself up on my knee, and stared at me with big brown eyes, as if she'd never seen a white person before. She probably hadn't. I felt like she could see through me, see that I was a fake. She knew I didn't belong. I couldn't look at the baby, her chubby hand sticky on my knee, little nails digging into the side of my leg. Barb leaned over and made cooing noises. The baby giggled. I knew she was laughing at me: the stupid, out-of-place white girl.

The priest paused, and Nando's parents stood to present a ring to Isabel. The priest said something, and Isabel and her friends shuffled their feet and giggled. People in the crowd laughed. My head swirled; my stomach churned. I wanted to get out.

Go back to the hotel. Walk on the beach like a normal person, sipping an umbrella drink. I belonged with the tourists, not these Mayans with their strange customs and weird churches. My face got all hot and prickly, like the time Fiona caught me lying about having a crush on Zach B.

Finally Isabel and her friends walked out of the church, and we all followed. People stood on the edge of the path greeting her like she was a queen, and I wondered if Nando modeled Muluc after his beautiful sister. I felt a little better in the fresh air, but I still wanted to go home: all the way home to Salt Lake City. It didn't help that my stomach growled loud enough for everyone to hear.

"Wasn't that so cool?" Barb said. "And that baby was so cute. Did you see that girl from lunch—the dancer? I'd like to have a special party when I'm fifteen. A mermaid party."

Yak yak yak.

The sun had dipped behind the trees, and everything glowed with warm light as we walked to an open-sided hut that overlooked the water. Isabel and her friends surrounded a small table in the center of the room while Nando's older brothers brought in an enormous three-tiered cake covered with big pink flowers and thick, loopy bows of frosting. Alfredo took a picture of Isabel blowing out her fifteen birthday candles. Everyone cheered and sang "*Las Mañanitas*"—just like in Mrs. Ruiz's class. Barb ran up to Isabel and handed her our stupid little present.

I tried to press against the wall and disappear.

Instead, I knocked over a case of Fanta Naranja soda. The

bottles rolled around on the floor. Clink. Clink. Clink. I tried to pick them up as fast as I could, but I knew everyone was staring at the crazy, clumsy white girl. An old man squatted down to help, smiling at me with his tobacco-stained teeth. I smiled back, but I wanted to cry.

Fortunately, musicians started playing, and everyone stopped staring at me and turned toward the music. A group of old men walked out to the center of the floor and began doing a real slow dance. So embarrassing! They looked like Dad doing his robot dance at family reunions. A small laugh popped out of my mouth. I searched the faces around me to see if anyone else was snickering, but everyone wore a solemn expression, as if they were still listening to the priest in church.

Then the musicians picked up the tempo, and Isabel danced with her father, sweeping around the floor like they were in a black-and-white movie. Other people joined in during the next song, and Nando, of course, danced with the girl from the restaurant.

I stood there, totally out of place.

Women from the village brought in trays of tortillas, chicken, beans, avocados, tamales, *taquitos*. So much food! Barb joined the people filling their plates. The smell of fresh, handmade tortillas tormented my empty stomach. But I couldn't eat something made in such conditions.

Barb scooped chicken into her tortilla. "This is amazing. The best ever. Even better than Dad's."

High praise from Daddy's Little Pet. Looking at all the food piled on Barb's plate, I realized that I hadn't eaten anything since breakfast.

While I'd been watching Barb feast, the girls had changed out of their formal gowns into their white embroidered dresses and were now dancing in their bare feet. Isabel wore the turtle earrings! A fast song started, and all the girls ran into the center of the room and twirled around, swinging their arms out wide. Nando's girl grabbed my hand and pulled me into the group, smiling at me with the kindest smile, but I pulled away.

I stood there like a lump, watching everyone else laugh and dance. What was stopping me? Why was I afraid of embarrassing myself? Fiona was thousands of miles away—she couldn't tell me I was "oh-so rhythm-challenged." I thought about how I climbed down that pyramid one step at a time. I just did it. Why couldn't I dance? I took a step toward the dancers. Then another. Nando rushed toward me, took my hand, and whirled me around, making me laugh at the dizzy feeling in my stomach.

A new song started, one full of drumbeats and a quick rhythm that made me think of Muluc for some reason. I closed my eyes and felt the music.

Around and around and around. I flung my arms wide like a little girl. The music matched my heartbeat. Time slowed. Peace wrapped me like my grandmother's hug. I belong. I belong. I belong. Everywhere, I belong.

When the song ended, I opened my eyes to see Nando smiling at me. "Let's get something to eat. *Mi mamá* just brought another batch of tortillas."

And I didn't shake my head no. I didn't even think about germs or whatever. I just thought about the delicious food, the happy laughter bouncing through the air, the friendship.

Barb continued dancing with the girls, but Nando and I walked outside, sitting on a flat rock overlooking the water, which shimmered with moonlight and shadows.

"The food is so good," I said, stuffing my face in a way that Fiona would call oh-so piggish, but I didn't care.

I chattered a bit about the food, but Nando had grown kind of shy, and I worried that I'd offended him again somehow.

"I want to apologize, Little Jaguar," he said. "I haven't been fair to you."

"What do you mean? I'm the one who was disrespectful. I'm totally sorry, and I'll never do anything like that again. I swear." I almost saluted, reminding myself way too much of Barb. "I mean, I understand how important it is to respect your culture."

"That's why I want to apologize." Nando stared out at the water. "I don't think I've been respecting your culture."

"My culture?" I couldn't even think what that was. Wearing the right clothes like Fiona? Listening to oh-so danceable music? Watching oh-so hilarious TV shows?

"I thought all Americans were the same." Nando smoothed the crease of his white slacks. "You know—big, loud, rich, throwing their money around, driving fast cars, living in mansions the size of a Cancún hotel, ordering Mexicans around."

I laughed. "You watch too much television."

Nando smiled. "Maybe. I do spend a lot of time at my cousin's house."

I thought about all the images of Americans on TV, and most of them weren't too flattering. Images of Mexicans weren't too flattering either. And all of it was wrong.

"The thing is," Nando said, "no one ever wanted to hear my stories before. Sure, the Americans want to joke about sacrifice, but then they want to go back to their hotels and sip fancy drinks by the pool. They like to climb the pyramid, take their photos, but they never think about the people who built such amazing temples. They never want to learn about the culture behind the climb."

I nodded. "I think I did start out feeling that way, but your story changed me." My cheeks burned as hot as the salsa. "I really like your story."

"I know. I've seen the thought you've put into the illustrations."

Now I felt like I'd turned the color of a thousand chilies—like Muluc that time.

"I've been thinking about things in a new way—like how my friends sacrifice people," I said.

Nando tilted his head. "You and your friends practice sacrifice?"

"No!" I suddenly felt so stupid, but Nando waited patiently for me to continue. "I'm talking about the way girls treat each other, like—"

Nando grinned. "American television?"

"Yeah, sort of, except for the private limos and stuff." I nudged his shoulder with mine. "That's totally not real."

"So tell me what is real, Little Jaguar."

And I did. I told him things I'd never told anyone.

We sat in the dark, watching the moon cross the sky, talking about friends and school, Mexico and America, until Barb came bursting outside, insisting that we come back and dance.

. . .

The next morning, I woke up swinging in my hammock, thinking about Muluc's story. I looked out through the walls of the hut and saw the first sparkle of sunlight skipping across the water of the lagoon-like cenote. Birds squawked in their tropical voices as a breeze rippled the leaves of the jungle canopy. I looked up at the tight artistic weave of palm fronds that formed the thatched roof. The fringed edges rustled in the wind. I had never experienced that kind of quiet: no cars rumbling, honking for carpool; no refrigerator humming; no air conditioner whirring. I'd never really thought about all the mechanical noises in a city, or even in my own house. I leaned deeper into the soft hammock, closed my eyes, and worked hard to make a memory.

But then Barb barged into the hut. "Kat! Come on." She tugged my hand. "Now!"

I followed Barb outside, where Nando held a tiny spider monkey in his arms.

"This one *is* a pet!" Barb rubbed the monkey's gray fur. "Wouldn't that be amazing to have a monkey for a pet?"

Before I could answer, the monkey reached out to me and climbed into my arms, wrapping its tail around my waist as if we'd always been friends.

"He likes you," Nando said, making Barb kind of pout — but only for a second.

"Nando's going to tell us the rest of Muluc's story. She escapes!"

We sat down, me still stroking the monkey's gray fur. As

Nando started talking, I reached up and held the monkey's soft, leathery hand. My head burst with all the things I wanted to remember about the *quinceañera*. Looked like I might be using that travel journal—in the way Mom wanted me to—after all.

"After the rain ceremony," Nando began. "On the day 6 Men . . ."

· · ·

THE DAY 6 MEN
Elderly Moon Goddess

Heavy gray clouds gathered in the sky two days after the ceremony. Breathing deeply, Muluc smelled rain coming. Balam had gone to the market to trade, and Macaw and Mol were in the jungle setting out vessels to collect rainwater.

To honor the gods, they had not spiced their food since before making the figures, so Muluc went to the garden to gather chilies. As she piled the peppers into her skirt, she kept looking behind her, feeling that someone was watching. A fly buzzed around the sleeping dog, a dry leaf skittered across the garden, and a pepper fell to the ground, but nothing else moved. Nothing hung in the branches above her. Maybe she was still upset by the sacrifice. Owls and snakes had haunted her dreams every night since then, and Quetzal's voice called to her in her sleep. She woke each morning as tired as when she'd gone to bed.

As Muluc stood to take the chilies into the house, she heard a hiss. Spinning around, she watched a snake slither from the plants she had been picking. She held her breath. The snake stopped in front of her and met her gaze. Muluc knew this snake.

Chilies spilling from her skirt, she ran down the road, away from the garden. Balam met her several paces down the road.

"Muluc? What is wrong?" he said. "Tell me."

Fear stole her voice.

"Did they see you? Did they find you?" he asked.

She shook her head, no, then yes.

Balam led her back into the hut. To Muluc, the tiny structure suddenly seemed so much more fragile, the walls practically transparent. Where could she hide? Under the thin sleeping mat? She searched for something to make her feel safe in the tiny space.

"Are you running from someone? Did someone come here? Have you seen any warriors? Are you the girl? Is he trying to steal you back?" Balam took a deep breath. "Kan is looking for a girl. A girl from Cobá." He paused. "Of course, a girl from Cobá." He put his head in his hands. "He is offering a big reward. Jade. People will remember you from the market."

"I saw a snake in the garden," Muluc whispered.

"Kan." Balam said. "He has a powerful *way*. His warriors say he can even change his form in battle."

Balam picked up a woven sack and threw in some corn kernels, dried peccary, and old tortillas. "We must leave, now," Balam said. "His men will be here soon."

"I want to say goodbye to your mother. And Mol," Muluc said.

Balam shook his head. "We have to go *now*."

Muluc looked at Macaw's mat, near the grinding stone. Tears filled her eyes. She bent her head and removed the jade pendant that hung from her neck, placing it under the mat.

"So she will remember me," Muluc said. "My name is engraved on it."

"We must go," Balam said.

Hand in hand, Balam and Muluc ran along the jungle trail, past the cenote where they gathered water, until the trail grew narrow, choked by vines and saplings. When Balam stopped to catch his breath, Muluc grabbed on to the trunk of a tree to steady herself.

"Balam," she said. "I must go alone."

"Never," he said.

"Your mother needs you," Muluc said. "And you don't need trouble if we get caught."

Balam didn't speak for a long time, but a tear dripped down his cheek.

"I can't let you go," he finally said.

"I don't want to leave you," Muluc whispered.

"But I'm not safe in Chichén. Snake—Kan—thinks he owns me." She touched Balam's cheek. "And you would not be safe in Cobá."

"I know," he said.

Rain began to fall, making music on the leaves high above. Balam and Muluc embraced until the water soaked their clothes; then Muluc continued on the narrow jungle path.

Alone.

Rivers of rain poured from the leaves, and Muluc's wet dress clung to her body. Her legs bled with scratches as she picked her way through the dense growth. She had left the path in case the warriors tried to follow her, but it was getting harder and harder to push through the tangle of vines surrounding her. Leaning against a tree, she stopped to rest, but water streamed down its trunk and over her shoulders, so she stepped away. Because Balam had not packed any tools in the sack, Muluc searched the ground for a sharp stone to help cut a path through the vines. She found two rocks and used one to chip a sharp edge onto the other, as she had seen Balam do.

The sky darkened, and rain continued to fall as Muluc chopped her way through the jungle, blisters burning her hands from working with the rough stone. Thunder thudded overhead, and lightning brightened the ground for just a moment.

"Thank you, Chac, for the rain," Muluc whispered to the sky. "Please help me find Cobá."

Long after night fell, Muluc stumbled through the darkness. Though she feared the spirits that haunted the jungle, she feared the warriors even more. A stream of rainwater washed over her feet as her trail opened into a clearing. Wind whistled through the high trees, almost like singing or crying, and a chill hung in the air. Muluc stopped. Was she hearing the Wailing Woman? She had heard stories about the ancient Wailing Woman who had been spurned by her lover and now wandered the woods, often disguising herself as a beautiful maiden to trick young men. Her cold touch left people unconscious, unable to speak. Or dead.

Muluc crouched against the trunk of a tree, waiting for her heartbeat to slow. Exhaustion caught up with her, and she fell asleep to the wailing of the wind above her.

• • •

THE DAY 7 CIB
Owl or Vulture, Death Birds of Night or Day

In the morning, the chill of Muluc's damp dress woke her. Her stomach rumbled, but what could she eat? She looked around the clearing and realized she'd fallen asleep in a cornfield. She was in someone's *milpa*! Muluc found a patch of melons growing among the corn. With her stone tool, she broke open a melon and slurped up the sweet fruit, letting the juice roll down her chin. Next she nibbled on an ear of corn like a mouse. Only when her hunger subsided did she wonder if she had been walking in circles.

A rough-cut path wound away from the *milpa*, but Muluc looked at the sky to see the position of the sun, and she headed away from the path, toward the rising sun. The trees did not grow so densely here, leaving her exposed in her tattered white dress. Had she wandered back into the outskirts of Chichén? Shaking away the thought, she continued walking, warmed—just a little—by the sunshine on her face.

"I've caught you." A man's voice echoed through the trees.

Muluc spun around.

"You're mine now," the man said.

Muluc crouched behind a low-growing palm.

"All mine," the man said.

A bird squawked. A quetzal—minus his shimmering green tail feathers—landed on a branch a few feet away. Muluc let out her breath, relieved, but then she saw the quetzal hunter walking toward her. She was sitting next to an empty trap! Hunched down, she crawled around the other side of the palm. A spiky frond snagged her hair, and the whole tree shook as she tugged herself free.

"What have we here?" the hunter said, raising one eyebrow. "A bird of another feather."

Muluc stood, heart pounding, and faced the man.

"A runaway." He smiled with brown-stained teeth and ran his hand over the top of his long, braided hair. A quetzal feather stuck out from behind his ear. "Let's see." He tilted his head and looked at Muluc. "You look elite."

"No," Muluc said. "Not in these rags." She opened her palms. "And my hands."

The man tapped his forehead, then pointed to hers.

"Just born that way," she said. "Mama says I should find a good husband with my long forehead." She tried to sound like a child.

"What brings you so far into the jungle, then?"

"I was searching for berries for dye," Muluc said. "Mama is weaving. I lost my way in the storm." Muluc paused as she tried to think of a way to ask about Cobá. "Are we close to . . ."

The man eyed the embroidery on her dress. "Chichén?"

Muluc's stomach sank.

"Not at all," the hunter said. "You've got quite a walk. If that is truly where you are going."

A flutter of birds rustled in the nearby brush, and the hunter rushed toward the sound.

"Wait here," he called back to her.

Muluc turned and ran, leaping over small bushes, forcing her body through tangles of vines, tripping over rocks. Ignoring the pain, she ran and ran and ran.

Doubled over with a side ache, Muluc clutched her stomach and tried to catch her breath, thudding down on the muddy ground next to a tall tree. Thick jungle completely surrounded her, so that she couldn't even tell where she had just been. No trace. At least the greedy quetzal hunter probably wouldn't bother searching for her. Muluc leaned her head back against the tree.

Above, in the elbow of a branch, she saw a circle of yellow and brown spotted fur. Jaguar! No, this creature was too small to be a jaguar. The cat lifted its head, and Muluc looked into its big round eyes: a little ocelot. Merchants in Cobá kept them as pets to keep mice out of the stored corn. After watching her for a few moments, the ocelot curled up again to sleep.

"Good idea," Muluc said. "I will wander at night like you do."

Muluc put her head on her sack and fell asleep, sunlight warming her like a blanket.

When the ocelot scratched its claws on the tree

branch, Muluc woke. Afternoon had faded to early evening; a light breeze fluttered through the darkening jungle like a whisper.

"Thank you, little Balam," she said, watching the ocelot stretch just as Balam did after a long day of work. "You also have a powerful *way*."

In the darkness, Muluc picked her way through the dense vines, using the rock to cut through some of them. The jungle had come alive with sound—not the friendly, bird-chirping sounds of daytime, but the sounds of the forgotten gods. A low growl hummed in the trees. Leaves crunched. Muluc's skin prickled with fear.

Do not panic, she told herself.

She stumbled through the trees onto a well-worn path. In the distance, a white glow stood out in the darkness. Was it a clearing awash in moonlight? An abandoned temple? She stepped closer, and the white glow seemed to stretch into the darkness. Straight, smooth, hard white cement. A white road, leading to Cobá!

A rush of air blew over her head in silence. In the moonlight Muluc saw the outline of an owl racing away from her. She screamed and ran back into the jungle to avoid the bird of death. Rough stones on the path cut through her damaged sandals. One shoe fell off. Still Muluc ran, ignoring the pain of sharp rocks cutting into her skin. Then . . .

Her feet left the ground, and she found herself falling deep into Xibalba, falling into the darkness. Reaching with her arms, she tried to grasp something. Anything. But there was nothing. Resigned, she stiffened her body, waiting for the guardians of the Otherworld to suck her below. But then she splashed into a cenote, sinking deep into the chilly water before fighting her way up to the surface. In the darkness she could hear bats beating their wings with a soft whap-whap.

She treaded water and waited for the Lords of the Otherworld.

* * *

THE DAY 8 CABAN
Moon Goddess, Crescent Phase

Sun filtered through the small opening of the cenote, and water shadows danced on the walls of the cavern. Thick roots from a ceiba tree above drank from the cenote; Muluc followed the roots with her eyes—they led to the top of the cavern, but not to the opening. Of course there wouldn't be an escape from the Otherworld. As her legs grew tired, Muluc held on to a slimy root to stay afloat. Maybe the Lords of Xibalba waited for people to die before taking them.

Hurting with hunger and shaking with cold, Muluc

lost her hold on the root. Water lapped against her chin, but she lacked the strength to keep herself afloat. Her eyes closed briefly, then longer. Snatches of dreams filled her thoughts. Sleep would feel so good. She allowed the water to cover her mouth. But then, just as she was about to succumb to the dark water, the sun shone directly over the cenote, lighting the cavern like a kitchen fire.

Shadows frolicked across the far wall, making shapes. Muluc remembered the child's game she used to play with friends, naming things in clouds, shadows, dust sprinkled across stone steps. With her laughter echoing throughout the cavern, she named things. Butterfly. Bird. Lizard. Crocodile. Cooking pot. What was that dark spot near the water's surface? Muluc blinked her eyes and stared hard at the spot that the sunlight never touched. Could it be a tunnel? The entrance to Xibalba? A surge of lightning raced through her body, and she gripped the vine with new strength.

"I won't let the gods take me," she whispered.

All night she clung to the wet root, shivering in the dark water.

• • •

Hi! Spent the night in Nando's village. Big party for his sister's 15th birthday.

Like a slumber party, except the whole village stays awake all night, eating, dancing & telling stories and stuff. In the a.m. we rappelled down into a cenote and swam in a cave.

Nando brought a flashlight and showed us all the formations.

Amazing!!! The Yucatán is connected by a whole series of underground rivers.

Ooops. I'm sounding like my dad.

Love Ya, Kat

P.S. See you soon.

• • •

I sat in a lounge chair by the pool, writing one last postcard to Fiona, but I wasn't sure that I'd send it. I kind of wanted to keep the photograph of the cenote in my travel journal. The ones I'd sketched didn't capture the magic of Nando's cool, quiet cenote. Maybe I *would* take that drawing class for my art elective next year, even if Fiona's Five all signed up for dance again. I reached for my sunscreen so I could put on a little extra, just to make sure. But then I didn't bother. Even if I had missed a spot, everyone needs a little vitamin D, right?

I tucked the postcard into my journal next to a rough sketch of Nando's sister dancing with her friends; they'd been so happy twirling around in their simple cotton dresses and bare feet. No one ranked anyone's Fashion Sensibility a 2.3 like my friends did. Mini-camp had already ended, but the private jokes would continue for months. Dumb stuff, really. Nothing as good as Muluc's story. I leaned back, closed my eyes, and enjoyed the warmth of the sun on my face.

Poor Muluc—stuck in that cold, dark cenote. She ran away to escape Snake, but she also protected Balam by making him stay behind. Fiona would beg me to escort her through the jungle and wouldn't even care if they sacrificed me once we got there—like she didn't care about making my short self go to basketball tryouts with her. Talk about oh-so humiliating! Spending time with Nando had made me think about what I wanted from friendship. He *did* like me, even though we came from different backgrounds and disagreed about so many things. And as much as I hated it at first, now I kind of liked the way he challenged me to think for myself, improve myself. He wanted me to be the best I could be, and maybe all friendships should be like that.

Barb swam to the edge of the pool and splashed me.

"Stop that, you pest!"

Barb pouted. "I can't believe Nando is making us wait for the end of the story. That's so mean."

"I told you he was mean," I said. "Think of poor Muluc. Hungry. Tired. Freezing cold. Nando is cruel."

"He is not."

"I know." I closed my eyes again. I can't believe I'm actually going to miss the guy! I opened one eye when Barb shouted out to Tanya.

"I brought us some drinks." Tanya handed Barb a frothy strawberry drink. "Two umbrellas."

"Yummy!" Barb sucked down practically half the drink. "And now I have exactly twenty-two umbrellas in my collection."

Tanya held up a virgin piña colada. "I brought one for you too."

"Uh, thanks."

I sipped the drink, worrying about poison for only a nanosecond. Old habit.

"So, Kat. About—" Tanya wrapped her blue-blond hair around her hand. "Can I?" She motioned to the empty lounge chair next to mine.

"Sure." I stopped myself from saying something snotty like "it's a free country." After some of Nando's stories about guerrilla uprisings, I wasn't sure it *was* such a free country.

"So . . . I'm sorry for—" Tanya blushed as pink as Barb's daiquiri.

"That's okay." No. Stop. "I mean. Thanks for apologizing."

"I'm not usually . . . It's just that things have really sucked with my parents, and moving, and trying to make new friends. And then I saw you, with a little sister who adores you and heaps of friends back home, and you seem so popular, and you're so cute."

I nearly choked on my piña colada. "What?"

"Come on. Josh totally has a crush on you. And Nando treats you like some kind of Mayan goddess or something."

"We're just friends." I pressed the icy cup against my cheeks. "And I'm *so* not popular."

"But you have so many friends." Tanya leaned close, gathering her hair over her shoulder, and whispered, "You didn't dye your hair blue to try to look ultra-fashionable."

"No." I tucked my hair behind my ear. "I cut it short because Fiona said we should all have 'oh-so' the same hairstyle. And I bought this shirt because Fiona said I should. And—" I explained the whole mini-camp situation and how Fiona chose her five best friends.

Tanya's eyes grew wide. "That's so not like you—all independent, kayaking by yourself, climbing pyramids illegally, jumping into cenotes, being all artistic with your sketchbook all the time."

I smiled at those memories. "Um, I kind of did all that stuff because I was afraid."

Tanya wrinkled her forehead, then laughed and kept laughing. At first I felt kind of insulted, but then it did seem funny, and I started laughing too.

"That doesn't make any sense." Tanya gasped for breath.

"I know!" I kept laughing, thinking that I hadn't laughed like this with Fiona in such a long time. Maybe never.

Over a second round of drinks, Tanya and I exchanged stories of stupid things we'd done for so-called "friends."

Barb swam over. "Are you guys ready now? Tanya, I've got to tell you what happens next."

"Guess I better—" Tanya sucked down the rest of her colada. "Thanks for the talk."

"You too," I said. "And thanks for putting up with Barb."

"Oh, you're so lucky. She's adorable!" Tanya slid into the water next to Barb. "Okay, so what happens next? She's at that Snake guy's house."

"Ooh! Ooh! The next part is so good—" They swam to the middle of the pool.

As I sipped my coconut drink, I thought about how Muluc had to travel far from home to realize what she wanted. What did I want now? I opened my journal to make a new list: "What I Want. Number 1: real friends who care about me as much as I care about them. Number 2: to be liked just for being me." I wasn't going to compete in Fiona's ongoing popularity contest anymore.

I guess my jungle crossing had changed me too.

The next morning, Tanya and I had to snag Barb by the back of her T-shirt to keep her from jumping off the bus to meet Nando by the side of the road. Nando climbed the steps extra slowly, fighting a smile.

"I think we should wait to finish the story. Maybe next time you visit Mexico."

The look of utter terror on Barb's face made us all laugh.

Nando sat next to me while Tanya and Barb leaned over the back of their seat. "So where did I leave Muluc?"

"In a cold, cold cenote!" Barb shrieked. "She might die."

"Come on, we've all watched enough American television to know that she's going to live," I said, glancing at Nando, who smiled back at me and continued the story.

• • •

THE DAY 9 ETZNAB
War God, Obsidian Sacrificial Blade

The next morning, butterflies played in the ferns growing at the opening of the cenote.

Muluc watched the colorful wings flapping: tiny, fluttering souls. Were they here to help her? Give her courage? She looked toward the tunnel, loosened her grip on the vine, and let herself sink into the water. Moving her stiff limbs, stretching, she swam to the tunnel. Uttering a short prayer, she decided to brave Xibalba rather than die waiting.

The water changed as she swam into its blackness. Colder. Smooth. The water smelled almost like rain falling on hot stone steps, and the memory of standing in the rain with her mother, thanking the gods for their gift, propelled her forward. Soon she lost her sense of direction. Up? Down? She swam with the ripple of current that ran through the water.

Rock formations tangled the cave as vines had tangled the jungle. Jagged spears of rock scraped her legs from below while thick ribbons of stone reached down into the water from above. At times, when her legs and arms tired, Muluc clung to these stony vines, losing track of time.

Her body shivered with teeth-chattering cold as she ran her hands along the walls of the deep tunnel to find her way. Sometimes the cave narrowed, and she had to swim underwater, feeling her way for long periods, longer than she had ever before held her breath. Finally she found a ledge and slept while the water flowed past.

. . .

THE DAY 10 CAUAC
Rain or Storm

Muluc startled awake after a restless dream about a quetzal devouring a snake. She saw light ahead! As she tried to rub warmth back into her arms and legs, the tunnel brightened around her with morning. Gathering all her strength, she swam toward the light . . . and found herself in another cenote. Not as far underground as the first, but still impossible to exit. Muluc tried to shimmy up a wet root, but she slid back down into the water again and again.

Soon raindrops began to fall into the center of the cenote. A waterfall crashed from the opening, echoing against the walls of the cavern like a thousand gods screaming. Was this the end? Muluc breathed in the earthy smell of the muddy water swirling around her. She spotted a small pink flower that had washed down with the rain. Crushing it into her wrinkled palm, she wept for her mother, father, baby brother, Balam, and even Quetzal. Would she ever see any of them again? Muluc had spent so much time thinking about all that she had taken for granted: her wealth, her education, her family . . . She'd acted as spoiled as an overripe melon!

The current of the river ran stronger, faster. Muluc felt around the edges for the entrance to the tunnel that would lead out of this cenote. She found a branch that had washed in with the storm, wrapped her arms over it, and floated, wondering if today would bring death.

The branch found the current, and Muluc sailed back into the darkness.

• • •

THE DAY 11 AHAU
Sun, Lord

Waking, Muluc squinted in the bright light and found herself floating in a watery grove of mangrove trees. Between the branches arching overhead, the sky glowed pink against soft white clouds. Had she entered the Otherworld at last? Through the clear water she saw colorful fish swimming in groups, like liquid butterflies. Butterflies were the souls of the dead in the Middleworld; maybe fish were the souls of the dead in the Otherworld. Didn't the Hero Twins turn into fish? A giant fish colored like a parrot scraped against her leg, but Muluc was too exhausted to even flinch.

The river widened, surrounded by high, rocky

cliffs as Muluc allowed the slow current to carry her. In the distance, waves crashed toward the river as it emptied into the sea. A sea turtle surfaced in front of her, then disappeared. Muluc peered into the water.

Below her swam a huge gray creature—as long as a small canoe. Muluc gripped the branch with all her strength, certain she would be taken by the gods now. The creature rolled on its back under the water and looked at Muluc with its huge hairy snout and large eyes. Everything went dark, and Muluc felt herself slipping under the water.

• • •

THE DAY 12 IMIX
Crocodile

"You have been with the Lords of Xibalba," a deep voice whispered in Muluc's ear. "Drink this." A firm hand lifted her head, and Muluc drank from the gourd, too tired to resist. The warm corn gruel tasted good, and she fell back and slept.

When the sun burned high in the sky, Muluc opened her eyes and found herself in a small hut. A coconut shell full of chopped fruits lay next to her mat. She gobbled every last bite, wondering how long it had been since she'd eaten. Footsteps. She pretended to sleep.

"Good, you've eaten," the voice said.

Muluc opened one eye. The oldest man she had

ever seen leaned over her—his skin wrinkled by time, but his eyes warm like chocolate.

"Am I in the Otherworld?" Muluc whispered.

"You have returned," he said.

"Did the monster take me?"

The man laughed, like leaves rustling in a warm breeze.

"The monster of which you speak rescued you." The man held his hand out to Muluc. "Come see."

Muluc's legs felt shaky as she walked outside onto the sand, but the sunlight felt luxuriously warm after the darkness that had chilled her bones. The man led her over to some rocks near the river. Stopping to pluck a few ripe papayas from a tree, he handed one to Muluc.

"Eat," he said. "Very good."

Quickly peeling the sweet fruit, she bit into the papaya.

As they walked to the edge of the water, the monster's face popped up. Muluc shrieked. The old man laughed and tossed a papaya into the water. The monster swallowed it, then rolled over like a puppy, playing.

"You met my manatee friend," he said, tossing another papaya into the water. "She is a gentle creature. She rescued you when you emerged from Xibalba." The man paused. "At least I think you came from the underground river."

"I—"

"May I read for you?" He put his hand on a small pouch hanging at his waist. "I am a daykeeper," he said.

"Like a priest?"

"Not so fancy. But I see things, know things."

He led Muluc over to a flat rock and spread out a colorful woven cloth. "You have been close to the gods. I can already feel the power."

He tapped his leg.

"Like lightning?" Muluc asked. "In your blood?"

"You feel it too," he said.

"I think so. Sometimes."

He bowed his head. "Do me the honor of asking a question."

"Will I find my home?" Muluc asked.

The daykeeper opened his bundle and spilled seeds, crystals, and small stones onto the cloth. He sorted the seeds and crystals into small groups, speaking the day names out loud. He looked up at her and grinned.

"You will see your family on thirteen Ik," he said.

"How long is that?"

"Today is twelve Imix."

"It is?" Muluc asked, not keeping the tears out of her voice. "I will see my family tomorrow? Tomorrow?"

"You have been on a long journey," he said. "But the gods have been with you."

"Where is the road to Cobá?"

"Rest today. Do not rush the gods." He said a prayer and packed up his bundle. "I will catch us some fish to eat," he said. "You will need strength for tomorrow's walk."

· · ·

THE DAY 13 IK
Wind, Breath, Life

Thirteen was a magical number.

The daykeeper had already started a fire and prepared some *atole* and tortillas by the time Muluc woke up.

Muluc thanked him for his kindness and food. "Please take this," she said, taking out her earring.

"It will be an honor to add it to my bundle," the man said. "A stone from the future queen of Cobá."

"What?" Muluc asked.

"You will see in time," he said. "You will know the power you possess."

He reminded her of the blind woman from the market, full of strange talk about the future. Muluc shook her head and said, "All I know is that I want to go home."

He pointed to a trail near the papaya tree. "Follow that path to the white road."

"Thank you." Muluc bowed deep.

"My honor," the man replied.

As Muluc entered the jungle, a cloud of butterflies, yellow, white, and blue, fluttered in front of her like a thousand souls from Cobá. All morning, she picked her way along the narrow path, careful to avoid stepping on the rocky outcroppings in her bare feet. The daykeeper's words echoed in her thoughts, and she thought about how her experience living as a slave — even a well-treated, beloved one — had changed the way she looked at commoners and their struggles. As a queen, she could have real influence! She couldn't wait to talk with her father and Quetzal — maybe they could make her story into a book. What if even commoners learned to read? As the lightning in her veins moved her legs faster and faster down the path, Muluc's thoughts grew bigger. Maybe she could convince Cobá's leaders to make peace with Chichén! Part of her wished for peace so that Balam could join her, but she knew now that she belonged with Quetzal. According to the daykeeper and the old blind woman at the market, the gods had plans for her.

At a fork in the path, Muluc stopped. What now? Squinting, she looked at the sun falling in the sky, trying to figure out which direction would lead her to Cobá. A blue jay landed on a branch a few feet down one path and sang out a few notes.

"I am listening this time."

Muluc ran down the path, following the blue jay all the way to the great white road.

"Thank you, kind bird," she said.

Kneeling down, Muluc opened a scab on her hand, dripping a few drops of blood onto the gleaming stones. Then she stepped onto the road as the sun dipped into the Otherworld and the sky grew dark, bringing to life the stars that told the story of creation and the Hero Twins. Muluc told herself the stories she had heard her whole life, even at Chichén, as she walked toward home.

Voices. Men laughing. Warriors!

But then one told a crude joke about an ancient king from Cobá, so Muluc smiled and continued walking.

"I see a girl on the road," one voice said.

"You're just trying to scare us."

"Maybe you can find yourself a wife," another joked.

"Look! It's a girl."

"Where?"

Three young men stood on the road ahead as Muluc strode confidently toward them.

"It's the Wailing Woman!" The three shrieked at once, scrambling off the road into the thick brush, cursing and screaming.

Muluc laughed as she ran toward the fires lighting the city of Cobá.

• • •

CHAPTER TEN

Finally we got to hear the end of the story! Nando had insisted that we reach Cobá at the same time as Muluc. With all the strange grinding metal noises the bus was making, I wasn't sure we *would* make it to Cobá, but I didn't bother adding anything to my list. Last night I'd been reading over my silly old list when Mom came into our room.

"Adding to the list?" Her voice sounded kind of sad.

"Naw. It's kind of stupid. I haven't seen any sharks, jellyfish, or flash floods. And the crocodiles I saw seemed more sleepy than dangerous."

"I'm glad." Mom looked over my shoulder as I paged through my sketches. "Those drawings are wonderful!"

"No, they're not."

"Kat. You've got real talent." She pointed to one. "That has to be that Snake warrior. Am I right?"

"Yeah." I felt like a total idiot because *my mom* was making me blush.

"You've got to learn to take a compliment, you know."

"I guess. Maybe I'll add that to my new list: 'Things I Want.'"

"Now that sounds like a worthy list." Mom squeezed my shoulder and walked back toward her own room. "But keep up your drawing too."

"Hey, Mom?"

Mom turned around, smiling. "What?"

"Thanks for taking us on this trip. It's been really great."

"I think so too." She smiled like a thousand-watt bulb.

In the seat in front of us, Barb leaned her head on Tanya's shoulder. With those two so cozy, we may have to arrange joint custody or something.

"Did she really become a queen?" Barb asked Nando. "Did she marry Parrot Nose—I mean Quetzal?"

"That is all for you to decide," Nando said.

"I think she did." I looked out my open window at a huge ceiba tree rising like a giant cross above the other trees in the jungle. "That's what she realized she wanted, right?"

"All of a sudden you have an opinion?" Barb said.

"It was a good story," I said. "A really good story."

"Thank you, Little Jaguar." Nando flashed his smile at me. "I didn't mind telling it to you. Much."

"And today we get to see Cobá!" Barb said. "I can't wait."

Before entering the city, Alfredo drove us around the lakes near Cobá. He tried to find a crocodile out sunning itself, but he couldn't. That was okay by me. I'd had enough of crocodiles. And I'm sure the crocs felt the same. Instead, Barb, Tanya, and I argued about seeing the exact spot where Muluc had been captured. Nando just sat there laughing at us.

Not much of Cobá had been excavated. Unexplored mounds dotted the sprawling city, and Barb was just about going crazy, wanting to become an archaeologist on the spot. Every pile of rocks contained some artifact from Muluc. We couldn't keep up with the tour, because Barb kept trying to climb things she shouldn't or get into things she couldn't.

I was dying to climb the big pyramid Nohoch — the highest pyramid in the whole Yucatán. And it was allowed this time!

We rented bicycles so we'd have time to pedal all the way out to the big pyramid. I couldn't believe that I was riding down the same long white roads that were in Muluc's story!

"Barb, let's go," I said.

Barb had stopped by the side of the road.

"Look at this temple," she said. "I see a doorway."

"Do not get off your bike!"

Too late. Barb had scrambled onto the rocky mound of a temple.

"Barb, get down here."

No good. Barb had disappeared into the rocks. Then I heard the loudest scream. I jumped up on the crumbling remains of a wall.

"Aaaaah!" I screamed.

A three-foot iguana stared at me from the doorway Barb had entered.

"Is it gone?" Barb asked in a shaky voice.

"Not even." The thing didn't budge. "It's as stubborn as you."

A few moments later the iguana sauntered down the rocks, disappearing into a grove of slender trees.

"You can come out now, Treasure Hunter."

"You go ahead." Barb rubbed the goose bumps on her arm. It was ninety degrees. "I don't think I'll do that again."

"You won't? Promise?"

"Not until I get a degree."

I got on my bike and rode through the quiet ancient city. So many buried secrets, so many buried stories. My heart sank when I saw the tour group coming back from the pyramid. Did I even have time to get there?

"You're going to like it," Dante said. "Very high."

"Yeah, Mountain Goat. This one was made for you," Josh said.

"Where's Barb?" asked Tanya. "Treasure hunting?"

"Yeah, she found something," I said.

"Really?" Tanya asked. "Something big?"

"If you like reptiles," I said.

"Ugh," the English girls moaned.

"Better hurry," Nando said. "The bus will leave in a half hour." He smiled at me. "Don't worry, I'll take care of our Little Thorn."

"Thanks."

I raced my bike along the path—just glancing into the green of the jungle. On the road a cloud of butterflies, yellow, white, and blue, floated in the air like petals.

"Hello, Muluc!" I shouted.

From the top of the Nohoch pyramid the whole world looked brand-new. I took out my journal and quickly sketched the view of trees engulfing the tops of weathered pyramids. I loved my journal now—except for that stupid old list! I ripped out the two pages of "Reasons Not to Go to Mexico," mentally saying good-bye to all those old fears and insecurities as I shredded them into confetti in my hands. Making an offering to myself, I tossed the bits of paper into the air, watching them flutter away like tiny white butterflies.

I stood with my arms held high, soaking up the greenness below me. I felt like a bird, as if I could jump off the pyramid and soar above the jungle canopy. A breeze cooled my skin, and I became part of the sky.

• • •

SALT LAKE CITY, UTAH

Dear Nando, Barb love love loves the jade stone you gave her.

She goes nuts about it being just like the one in Muluc's necklace. She's in treasure heaven. Thank you for the little jaguar you carved for me—my own little balam. It's so cute! And it WILL remind me to be brave. Thanks for everything else too. I can't thank you enough, really. I'm going to miss you so much.

Promise me you'll write. Often.

Love, Kat, aka Little Jaguar

P.S. Are you still thinking about writing down Muluc's story? I promise to illustrate it!

P.P.S. When are you going to visit us????

• • •

AUTHOR'S NOTE

I vividly remember when I was six years old and climbed down a steep, dimly lit stone staircase to the elaborately carved tomb of King Pacal, who became ruler of the kingdom of Palenque when he was just twelve years old. My biology professor dad had taken our family to Mexico on a research trip. We stayed in small villages, where women washed their clothes in the river and carried their clean laundry home folded neatly on top of their heads! I loved the marketplaces, where vendors sold all kinds of exotic, ripe-smelling fruit, crafts, and even live chickens.

I wrote *Jungle Crossing* after another family trip. This time I was a grownup, traveling with my husband, my daughters, and their grandmothers. We climbed pyramids in the Yucatán region in the ancient cities of Tulum, Chichén Itzá, and Cobá. We also spent time in a modern Mayan village and even swam in an underground river, bumping into the stony stalactites tangling the cool, dark water. Kat's story follows many of my own travels.

The story of Muluc comes entirely from my imagination, but it is based upon the things I've learned by reading history, archaeology, anthropology, sociology, mythology, and memoirs, as well as my own experiences. As tourists, we saw the elaborate carvings of Mayan royalty in the temples, pyramids, and tombs. One of the stele carvings found at Cobá depicts a queen. Since many of the carvings also show slaves, I imagined what would happen if a royal girl from Cobá suddenly found herself captured by warriors from the rival city of Chichén.

I also wanted to show readers that descendents of the ancient Mayans, like Nando, still live in Mexico today. Although the Spanish conquistadors devastated Mayan culture by burning books, enslaving people, and bringing disease and death, many of the Mayan people survived. Their descendents are now scattered throughout Mexico, Central America, and the United States. In fact, if you're of Hispanic heritage, there's a chance that your ancestors once lived in the great ancient Mayan kingdoms.

ACKNOWLEDGMENTS

Thanks first to my daughters, Emma and Sophie, who inspired me to begin my writing journey.

Thanks to my writing group, especially Kelley and Susan, for helping me make it through the thorny tangled times.

Thanks to my family, whose support for this book I will always treasure: my grandpa, Ted; my mom, Rondi; my dad, Dave; my step-mom, Stephanie; my mother-in-law, Marcia; my brother, Ethan; and my sister-in-law, Colleen.

Thanks to my husband, Mike, with whom I've shared so many adventures (with many more to come).

Thanks to my agent, Ted Malawer, for his enthusiasm and all those initial excavations!

And finally, a pyramid of thanks to my editor, Julie Tibbott, who worked like a literary archaeologist to help me uncover the heart of the story.

GLOSSARY

altar a large stone used for religious rituals and offerings

amigas friends

amor love

atole a warm cornmeal drink

balam jaguar

banditos bandits

bienvenido welcome

bisabuela great-grandmother

bonita beautiful

bonjour hello (French)

buenos días good morning

ceiba tree a sacred tree at the center of the Mayan universe, believed to reach from the Otherworld into the heavens

Chac the Mayan rain god

Chac Mool stone statues of a reclining human figure, used in ancient Mayan rituals, including sacrifice

chérie dear (French)

Chichén/Chichén Itzá an ancient city located in the northern center of the Yucatán Peninsula in Mexico

chicleros men who collected sap from the zapote tree that was then used to make chewing gum

coati a small, racoon-like mammal

Cobá an ancient Mayan city located in the Yucatán

con with

copal a smoky-scented incense made from tree sap, used as offering to the gods. Also known as *pom*

daykeeper a person who kept track of the calendar days, performed rituals, and read the future

digging stick a long, pointed stick used by Mayans to plant corn

¿Estás listo? Are you ready?

flint a hard gray rock, used to make weapons; also starts fires; used in sacrifice

frijoles beans

gracias thank you

Great Star Venus

Hero Twins the brothers at the center of the Mayan religious book *The Popul Vuh*

Hola hello

impatiens a plant with pink, red, or white flowers; used to make dye

incense burner a sculpture used to burn incense for religious worship

jade a hard green stone that symbolized maize, water, sky, and life; often used for jewelry

kan snake

Kulkucan/Great Vision Serpent represented by a feathered serpent; a god of war

"Las Mañanitas" the Mexican birthday song

lip plug a stone jewel placed in a lip piercing

maize god a beautiful young god associated with the Hero
   Twins myth

Middleworld the earth's surface, where people and animals live

me llamo my name

milpa a small field containing several crops, including corn,
   beans, squash, and melons

mol monkey

muy very

obsidian a dark, glassy lava stone used to make weapons and
   mirrors

offering a gift given to the gods

Otherworld/Xibalba a scary place under the surface of the earth
   that could be entered by a cave or standing water; ruled by
   gods of death and other lords

peccary a wild pig

pom a smoky-scented incense made from tree sap; burned in
   Mayan religious ceremonies

por favor please

prima female cousin

profesor teacher

pulque alcoholic beverage often used in religious ceremonies

quinceañera a girl's fifteenth birthday tradition that celebrates
   God, family, friends, music, food, and dance

ramon a bright green nut often gathered when crops failed

señor sir

scribe a person who writes books by hand

sí yes

skull pressing a practice used to create an elongated forehead, thought to be very beautiful

Snake Mountain a carving depicted in Chichén Itzá, believed to represent an aspect of creation

sun disk a symbol of war

tamale steamed corn dough filled with meat or vegetables and wrapped in cornhusks

taquito a rolled-up tortilla, stuffed with meat filling and deep-fried

trumpline a strap attached to a backpack that is worn over the top of the head to ease the burden of carrying heavy loads

turista tourist

turquoise a greenish-blue stone used for jewelry

uno one

vámonos Let's go!

Wak-Kan, Six Snake another name for the World Tree

way wizard-like power

World Tree a symbol of the center of the Mayan universe

Xibalba/Otherworld a scary place under the surface of the earth that could be entered by a cave or standing water, ruled by gods of death and other lords

Websites for *Jungle Crossing*

The Mayan people developed a complicated calendar system that was more accurate than the one we use today. To learn more about it go to www.mayacalendar.com or www.michielb.nl/maya/astro.

To read more about the Hero Twins story, go to www.mayas.mr-donn.org/herotwins.html.

To learn more about the archaeological site of Chichén Itzá, go to www.wikipedia.org/wiki/chichen_itza or www.smm.org/sln/ma.

To learn more about the archaeological site of Cobá, go to www.wikipedia.org/wiki/coba or www.smm.org/sln/ma.

To learn more about the archaeological site of Tulum, go to www.wikipedia.org/wiki/tulum or www.smm.org/sln/ma.

To learn more about Mayan gods and goddesses, go to www.mayankids.com.

Do you think you might want to be an archaeologist someday? Go to www.digonsite.com for all kinds of fun information about ancient cultures around the world.

SYDNEY SALTER's fascination with Mayan culture started when she was six years old and climbed down a steep, dimly lit stone staircase to the elaborately carved tomb of King Pacal, a ruler of Palenque. Visiting Mayan ruins, walking through fragrant Mexican marketplaces, and chasing lizards in the jungle ignited Sydney's imagination and led to writing *Jungle Crossing*. Sydney lives in Utah with her husband, two daughters, two cats, and two dogs. She loves reading, writing, cooking, and traveling—especially to Mexico. She is also the author of *My Big Nose and Other Natural Disasters* and *Swoon at Your Own Risk*.

www.sydneysalter.com